THE LEGS OF THE LAME
And Other Stories

by
Hugh Garner

Borealis Press Limited
Ottawa, Canada
1976

PS
8513
A72L4
1976

Published with assistance from Canada
Council and Ontario Arts Council

ISBN 0-919594

Borealis Press Limited
9 Ashburn Drive
Ottawa, Canada K2E 6N4

Printed and Bound in Canada

THE LEGS OF THE LAME
AND
OTHER STORIES

Books by Hugh Garner:

Storm Below, novel, 1949
Cabbagetown, novel, 1950
Waste No Tears, novel, 1950
Present Reckoning, novel, 1951
The Yellow Sweater, short stories, 1952
Silence On The Shore, novel, 1962
Hugh Garner's Best Stories, short stories, 1963
Author! Author!, humorous essays, 1964
Men and Women, short stories, 1966
Cabbagetown, hard cover reprint, 1968
The Sin Sniper, mystery novel, 1970
A Nice Place To Visit, novel, 1970
Violation Of The Virgins, short stories, 1971
Three Women, one-act stage plays, 1973
One Damn Thing after Another, autobiography, 1974
Death In Don Mills, mystery novel, 1975
The Legs Of The Lame, short stories, 1976
The Intruders, novel, 1976

ACKNOWLEDGMENTS:

My thanks to Mr. Robert Weaver, Head, CBC Radio Arts, who purchased the following stories, which were read on the CBC radio network program *Anthology*.

"The Legs Of The Lame," "Moving Day," "A Walk On Y Street," "Losers Weepers," "A Short Walk Home," "See You In September," "One For The Road," "Station Break." "Jacks Or Better, Jokers Wild," "The Man With The Musical Tooth," "Wait Until You're Asked," and "The Customer Is Always Right."

My thanks also to the editors of the following magazines which first printed these stories:

Canadian Forum, "Jacks Or Better, Jokers Wild"; *The Canadian Fiction Magazine*, "See You In September"; *Catalyst IV*, "Wait Until You're Asked"; *Journal Of Canadian Fiction*, "A Walk On Y Street," "A Short Walk Home," and "Station Break"; *Miss Chatelaine*, which also printed "A Short Walk Home"; *New Canadian Stories*, "Losers Weepers"; *Quarry*, "The Man With The Musical Tooth"; *Queen's Quarterly*, "One For The Road"; and *Tamarack Review*, "The Legs Of The Lame."

CONTENTS

.

THE LEGS OF THE LAME

It was only a two hour trip, and I was feeling good. The best two meetings, in Kingston and Carleton Place, had gone off well, and Kingston, being semi-big time, had received quite a play from the media, so that our attendance the next week in Toronto was almost an assured success.

Behind us was the preliminary build-up, beginning with small churches and fraternal halls, and then progressing to war memorial auditoriums and centennial centres. Despite Clay's crazy desire to meet all his obligations, and my trying to impress on him the necessity of honoring only the big towns and their consequent bigger audiences, that he insisted on calling "congregations," we were still moving up, and so were our bank accounts.

I hadn't been able to talk him out of it, and so the evening before we'd held a "visit," in a skating rink in Perth. We'd had a fair-sized audience and the handle had been ten times what it used to be three months before. We'd drawn the faithful from Smiths Falls and other towns around, but to me it was like Sinatra or Dylan playing Belleville.

Clay was quiet, sitting there beside me in the front seat as the Caddy glided along at eighty coming west on Ontario No. 7 after midnight.

"Perth was pretty good for its size," I said to Clay.

"Yes."

"It sure beat both Cornwall *and* Sherbrooke."

"They're largely Roman Catholic cities," he answered, staring straight ahead through the windshield. "Perth had a lot of born-again Christians."

Paula Dunwoody and her husband Fred, sitting in the back seat, were quiet now, and I knew one of them must be asleep. Paula played the harmonium we were pulling behind us in the small covered trailer with the JESUS HEALS signs on its sides. The trailer was about the size of a medium U-Haul and carried, along with Paula's harmonium, our bags and a rack holding Clay's new wardrobe.

I slowed the car as we passed through Kaladar, then let it ease up to eighty again on the open highway. Except for a few tractor-trailers there was very little traffic, and through my open window I caught the spring scent of coniferous trees and an occasional whiff of

1

something like buckwheat. The beam of our lights picked out the stretches of bush and abandoned sapling-growth fields as we raced past them.

"This part of Ontario should never have been cleared for farms," I said. "Most of them have been abandoned for years."

"Yes," Clay said.

Fred Dunwoody asked, "How much farther to Peterborough, Gordon?"

"Sixty-five, something like that," I said. "Is Paula asleep?"

"Like a baby. I think I'll take forty winks myself."

I glanced over at Clay and saw he was still wide awake, staring straight ahead. Usually a "visit," which was what we called our faith-healing meetings like the one in Perth, exhausted Clay, and he would sleep all the way to our next motel stop. Tonight though for some reason he was wrapped up in sleepless thought. I figured he was thinking of his wife Eileen and his two small kids back in Bridgewater, Nova Scotia. They'd been with us for the two days we took off from the tour in Quebec City, and for some reason he hadn't been the same enthusiastic Clay Burridge since we'd left Quebec.

I'd booked us three units in a motel just east of Peterborough, where we were holding a two-night visit beginning that evening. When it was possible I always got us lodgings outside the towns we appeared in. Most people don't know this, but an evangelical celebrity, even a minor one like Clay, is bothered constantly by women fans. It had only taken me the first two weeks I'd been Clay's business manager and advance man to catch on to that fact. The women as a group were older than the ones that used to bug the rock group I'd managed, but there's a mixture of sexuality and religion in a successful evangelist and faith-healer. A person like Billy Graham must have to beat them off with clubs.

I'd been trying to figure out Clay Burridge now for three months, but still couldn't. He didn't smoke, drink or swear, and he was completely faithful to Eileen Burridge. Not that he couldn't have had plenty of women, as I say, but he turned them all away politely.

The way I got myself tied in with Burridge is a story in itself.

It was by attending a meeting of his during one of his first big visits, in Halifax. I'd just been left as high and dry as it's possible to get

2

down there by a rock group I'd put together we called "The Flack." I know it wasn't a catchy name like "Three Hits And A Miss," but did you ever stop and think what a lousy name "The Beatles" is? I know that the first time I heard it I thought of little black bugs crawling across a floor. Anyhow, all I'd got from "The Flack" was plenty of woe and a little more than my hotel room and bar bills. My girl vocalist took off on a speed trip with my drummer and my car, which ended up as a write-off near Boston. That disbanded the outfit, and I paid the other two members' plane fares back to Toronto. I guess I attended Clay Burridge's meeting as a penance for my stupidity.

First of all let me say that before I took him over Clay's meetings were strictly from hunger. His approach to the whole soul-saving, faith-healing business was an evangelical road to the welfare office. Take the way he dressed for instance. Not plain folks like Oral Roberts or no-nonsense religio-commercial like most of the successful preachers on the circuit, but in a way that appealed only to the lowest hayseed denominator in his audience.

After the first meeting I attended was finished I went backstage and met Clay and Fred Dunwoody. They were leery of me at first, but I trotted out my tattered credentials, and they invited me to Clay's hotel room, which wasn't in the Nova Scotian or the Lord Nelson. I began right away to criticize his stage appearance, the general downbeat tone of the whole gig, and after some coaxing on my part which got them to tell me, the unrealistic financial split he'd made with the theatre owners. I was afraid that Clay or Dunwoody would throw me out of the room, but they listened to me politely.

I told them, "Who's going to believe a preacher who still wears a fancy buckskin jacket and a ten-gallon hat? You're not out to prove that you're a second Nova Scotia cowboy like Hank Snow. You've got to put yourself over as a dedicated, educated preacher, not as a sideshow freak saving the souls of the rural poor. You're a person with a genuine gift from God who is willing to share it and your message with everybody. You've got to make your audience − all right congregation then − believe in you, not only with hope or religious faith but with their intelligence. You've got to get out of the dimes and into the dollars."

"I didn't have much of a formal education, Mr. Beaton," Clay said, in the soft but unbelievingly earnest way he speaks; the way it had actually gripped me in my seat in the half-filled theatre. "I'm dedicated though. There's nothing phony or showbiz about my Christianity, and nothing untruthful about my belief in the healing powers of Jesus Christ. I may sometimes find myself doubting my qualifications to act as His healing surrogate, but my attempts to bring His healing grace down to the poor unfortunates who seek it are real. As for a wider audience – not for me but for the Lord – I'd welcome that. It has nothing to do with either dimes or dollars however."

I believed him as you'd have believed him too if you'd been in that small hotel room that night. There wasn't the slightest doubt in my mind that the man was telling the truth. Hell, he was that rarest of individuals, an incorruptible one!

Anyhow, in a couple of days Clay Burridge and Dunwoody visited me at my motel and we drew up a simple agreement making me Clay's business manager and advance man. Straight percentage of the gate after expenses.

We had to make the changes in his image gradually, for going too fast would have lost him what few followers he had then. First off we had to change his public picture, and so before leaving Halifax I had him trade in his old panel truck for a second-hand sixty-nine Cadillac, that he bought on time. He made the deal himself, in his own name; I wasn't trying to rip him off.

The beginning of our tour took us up Nova Scotia's Eastern Shore, to places like Sheet Harbour, Port Dufferin, Ecum Secum and Liscomb, then inland to Aspen and up to Antigonish. It was a strictly hungry itinerary scheduled by Clay and Fred Dunwoody before I joined them. It allowed me though to make some changes in the performance itself. Man, Clay's act had more kinks in it than a snake fence. Besides leaving Halifax in the Cadillac I'd work as far ahead of the show as I could, spreading the word and arranging meeting places and cut-rate accomodation.

I stole an idea from Billy Graham, and wherever I could I arranged "participatory partnerships" with local fundamentalist preachers. At times they were deep-dip Baptists, other times evangelicals, and at least once before we kissed Nova Scotia goodbye the minister was a genuine get-down-on-the-floor-and-pray Holy Roller. There "partner-

4

ships" paid off in attendance for both the local preacher and Clay Burridge, and the amount of the handle we pulled in.

I succeeded too in getting Clay to change his personal appearance. At first it was the substitution of a Sears mail-order dark suit for his Buffalo Bill buckskins, and before we hit Sackville, New Brunswick we'd got rid of his ten-gallon hat. And if you think it's easy to separate a let's-play-cowboy Maritimer from his Stetson, try it sometime.

In the bigger towns and small cities like New Glasgow, Pictou and Amherst I received the co-operation of some of the leading Protestant clergymen, not all of them fundamentalists. The word of Clay's coming was spread by what I can only call a Christian underground telegraph. By now we were booking our visits into war memorial auditoriums and centennial sports arenas.

Where Clay had been satisfied at first with small high school gyms and Sunday schools, now I was counting the gate in hundreds, some "partners" supplying us with a back-up choir and orchestra, meaning we could leave Paula Dunwoody's harmonium in the trailer. Our first trailer had been a rented one, but the second, that served us right up into Ontario, was a gift from an old man who'd hauled hay in it for years from the salt marshes near Tidnish. He presented it to Clay for curing his arthritis. We had it fixed up and painted in Saint John.

From Sackville on I made up the itinerary, having to talk both Clay and Dunwoody out of heading through Moncton and up the New Brunswick North Shore. I pointed out to them that there were ten times as many Protestants up the St. John River valley and in towns like Sussex and Woodstock, to say nothing of Saint John, than in the Acadian towns on the shore.

We did real good in Saint John, in four services making three times as much as we'd made on the whole tour up to then. Not only was I planning the trip and doing the advance work, but I'd programmed each service carefully with the help of the participating clergymen. If religious meetings can be called boffo successes, we were succeeding by then.

"What place is this?" Clay asked, as we ran through a village at forty. His voice from beside me jarred me out of my thoughts about the trip so far and about the future, which was as enticing to me as the Pearly Gates.

5

"Marmora," I told him. "We've got another thirty-five miles or so."

"I've been thinking about the couple of days we stayed in Quebec City, Gordon," he said.

"Yeah, Clay, it was great for you having Eileen and the children with you. Don't forget they're flying up to Toronto next week."

"I'm looking forward to it," he said. I could see him shifting on the seat and staring back at the Dunwoodys.

"They're both asleep," I said.

"Yes." After a minute he said, "I've been thinking of Eileen and the children, naturally, but lately I've been thinking of something else."

I nodded. "I know, Clay. I could feel it."

"Remember the day Eileen and I went out to Ste. Anne de Beaupré, to the shrine?"

"Yes, I remember."

"It's a magnificent place, Gordon."

"Maybe some day you'll have a shrine like it, Protestant of course, down near Bridgewater," I said, wondering what he was driving at.

"No, Gordon, I wasn't thinking of anything like that."

"What then, Clay?"

"I told you that I'd had a visit with the vicar there, a middle-aged priest called Father Lanphier."

"Yeah?"

"He'd never heard of me, of course, but we had quite a talk. Every pillar of the basilica is ringed almost to the ceiling with crutches, leg braces, wheelchairs, every prosthetic device made to help the maimed and crippled."

"The Catholics go for that kind of show," I said.

He said nothing, but I knew he was staring at me.

"There was the man in Truro who walked out of your meeting carrying his crutches under his arm, and how about the old lady who pushed her own wheelchair up the aisle at the end of the Fredericton visit?"

As if he hadn't heard me Clay said, "Father Lanphier told me that out of the many hundreds, thousands, who have visited the shrine and prayed to God through Ste. Anne for a miraculous cure, and out of the great many who have claimed to be cured, and have left their crutches behind as a testament, only a very few have been authenti-

6

cated as genuine cures by their clerical and medical committees."

I didn't know what to say.

"The vicar told me that most of those claiming miraculous cures had been temporarily relieved of their pain, and had been able to walk without help temporarily because their crippling diseases had been psychological to begin with. Either that or their profound faith in the miracles of Ste. Anne had induced a hysteria that made them *believe* they were cured. Unfortunately, Father Lanphier said, in most cases this had not been so." "

I had to say something so I said, "But, Clay, how about those that were authenticated as cures? And even if they weren't cured, think of all the people whose spirits were raised by praying at the shrine, just as you have raised people's spirits at all your visits. You've given people *hope*.

"Yes, Gordon, hope that may last a few hours or until I've left them behind, then what? And what of those who substitute a laying on of hands for the real medical attention they should be getting? What must they think of a preacher who promises them miracles but only gives them a few hours respite from their pain and fears instead?"

"But you're offering them Christian service, Clay. You're leading them to the Lord, and — "

"Nobody needs a preacher to lead them to the Lord," he said. "I can only point out the way; only show them the efficacy of prayer. Only give them hope that the Lord Jesus Christ will hear them."

I remembered one of his biblical homilies and I said, "Clay, since I met you I've never heard you claim to heal anyone, but only intercede between your penitents and God. I remember you saying, "And I was strengthened as the hand of the Lord my God was upon me."

"Yes, Ezra seven, twenty-eight. Haven't you ever thought, Gordon, that I must be the most conceited man in the country to think that this hand — " He stuck it in front of my face so that I swerved the car to see the road ahead. " — represents the hand of God?"

I didn't answer him, but drove on. It was the only time since meeting him and working with him that I'd discussed his healing powers with him. What can you do when a preacher, or a performer for that matter, loses his egotistical faith in himself. It's the end of the road. I saw not only the hopes and faith of thousands destroyed but a fortune going up in smoke. It wasn't that we were stealing from the people who were beginning to flock to our visits; they *wanted* to come, and made their often painful way many miles to have Clay Burridge lay his hand on them and intercede between them and God. Watching him over the months had even converted *me*.

I drove on through the small deserted towns of Havelock and Norwood, wondering what I could do to bring Clay back to his senses. I thought at one stage that an appeal to his obligations to his wife and children might do it, but realized it would be like asking a movie star to give up the glamor and glitter of Hollywood because he felt his acting was ripping off the movie patrons.

The next morning, late, I woke up in my motel room and answered a knock at the door. It was Fred Dunwoody.

"Morning, Fred, what time is it?"

"Nearly eleven, Gord."

I remembered my conversation in the car with Clay. Panic-stricken for a moment I asked, "Anything the matter, Fred?"

"No. Not really."

"Where's Clay?"

"In his room. He's eating breakfast."

"What's up then?"

"Nothing, Gord, I just thought you might have quite a lot to do in the city this afternoon. You told me yesterday you had to see the arena people and the minister who's supplying the orchestra and choir. I didn't want you to sleep in."

"No. Thanks, Fred, for waking me. How's Clay acting this morning?"

Dunwoody gave me a bewildered look. "Acting? He's fine, as well as *I* can make out."

In utter relief I said, "Good, Fred. I'll get shaved and dressed and drive into town."

The minister who was supplying the choir and orchestra was a young man with a beard who wore a huge Christian medallion around his neck over his denims. When I met him he was smoking a long filter-tip cigarette and there was a bottle of Australian sherry on his desk. I don't cotton much to hippie or would-be hippie preachers, and I certainly

8

don't like people who are unsophisticated enough to flaunt bottles of *Australian* sherry instead of the real thing.

After a long give and take about the splitting of the gate, which he tried to up in his favor despite the telephone agreement we'd reached days before, he said, "I don't hold with nineteenth century Methodist hymns. I think the orchestra and choir should open with a medley of modern songs."

"You mean rock-'n-roll?"

He looked at me, and I realized that modern rock was the only kind of music he knew had ever existed.

It was too late to slough him off now. "Okay, Rev.," I said. "But don't forget we insist on *Put Your Hand In The Hand* when Clay Burridge begins his healing."

"Sure."

"How big is your choir?"

"Forty. Thirty girls, ten young men."

"Great. What kind of an orchestra have you, Reverend Smoker?"

"The usual. Six pieces, piano, drums, base and three guitars."

"No brass or woodwinds though?"

"As I said, the usual."

"You've got a copy of the order of the service. Remember you have no more than ten minutes on stage yourself."

"I've read it carefully. We conduct services all over the holiday country during the summer, and our musical group has performed as far away as Charleston, West Virginia."

"Okay."

"Can I offer you a tot of sherry, Mr. Beaton?" he asked. I'm only a minor league hustler, but I know the difference between "can" and "may," and I hate non-sailors using words like "tot" or "good-o."

"No thanks," I said, shaking his hand and getting out of his poster-decorated parsonage.

The arena people were much easier to deal with, and before I left the arena-manager's office we had things laid out just fine.

There were the usual handful of people waiting at the stage door of the arena when we arrived. Clay autographed several Bibles and New Testaments, gave a couple of private benedictions, and then repeated the biblical verse he always did on such occasions. "Heal me, O Lord, and I shall be healed; save me, and I shall be saved: for thou art my praise."

Fred Dunwoody went off to find the arena manager and to station the ushers, while Clay and I went to his dressing room, I carrying his fresh-laundered white shirt, blue suit and subdued dark blue necktie. Paula Dunwoody remained outside the dressing room, warding off callers by telling them that the Reverend Clay Burridge was meditating before the service began. Later on she'd apply Clay's light make-up.

Clay changed his clothes and sat at the makeshift dressing table reading his Bible, while I looked through the papers checking the advertising and making sure they had the time of the visit correct. I not only had the Peterborough *Examiner*, but papers from Lindsay, Cobourg and Port Hope. From the tiers of seats ringing the arena and the rows of temporary chairs placed on the arena floor itself I could hear the arrival of the crowd that promised to be the biggest one we'd ever had.

"This is going to be a big one, Clay," I said as I got up to leave the dressing room.

"Yes. I can hear the crowds coming in," he said.

I could detect no difference in his attitude from all the times before. "Gook luck, Clay."

"Thanks, Gordon. The Lord be with us."

I took my place in an empty seat at the side of the built-up stage next to the wide entrance from backstage. Already the arena was almost jammed to capacity, the tiered seats and those temporarily placed on the floor. The ushers were those regularly employed by the arena management. On stage the choir, the girls and women wearing white blouses and skirts and red blazers, the young men white shirts and trousers and red blazers, were already in place, forming an eye-catching red-and-white background to the stage itself. The small orchestra, mikes wired to the sound system, were in position at the other end of the stage. The sight of the choir surprised me; after meeting with the Reverend Smoker I'd expected something – well, something not as professional looking.

A middle-aged fat man in a dinner jacket came along the entrance-way from backstage and after a brief glance at the audience climbed the steps, walked to a spot behind the green-fronted lectern, and raised a baton. The audience hushed momentarily, then the orchestra and choir broke into their opening medley. It wasn't what I'd expected, but was much better. A sort of mixture of Mantovani and the Mormon Tabernacle Choir playing and singing a softened version of Broadway standards. The kind of happy, expectant music I'd been hoping to hear since the early days in Sheet Harbour and Pictou.

When the music finished it seemed a little strange not to hear a burst of applause, and it took me a second or two to realize that the audience was really a religious congregation and that applause, to them, would have been like clapping in church.

The introductory music was followed by an old man in clerical clothes who thanked the crowd for its attendance and gave a short talk about the resergence of religion among the youth, sweeping his arm behind him at the members of the choir.

The old minister, who I gathered from my notes must have been an Anglican canon named Dumphrey, one of the participating partners, finished his talk on time and left the stage. With superb timing the choirmaster raised his baton, the congregation rose to its feet with a shuffling of clothes and chairs, and all broke into a beautiful modern hymn, unknown to me until then. To say that it shook me up would be an understatement.

There were several verses to the hymn, and the congregation seemed to know them all, and continued to its end.

The choir then furnished a vocal counterpoint to a girl soloist who sang *Abide With Me* in a beautiful soprano voice. She was no longer finished than I noticed that the Reverend Smoker had taken his place, unobtrusively at the lectern. He was a much different young man than the one I had met that morning at his church. Dressed now in a light gray business suit with a clerical collar he spoke softly and reverently into the microphone.

I can still remember some of his sermon. "There is no such thing as new life . . . life was and always will be, and it is not known what life is. There is only one life. The everything is life, the universe, the whole, the all is one life. We give that life a name and that name is God . . . . "

When he finished I glanced at my watch, and he'd ended in precisely ten minutes. For one mad moment I wished I'd given him more time. The Reverend Smoker was followed by the whole congregation singing another hymn, but by now I was so excited by the wonderful way things were going that I don't remember which one it was. I went backstage to Clay's dressing room, where Paula was applying the finishing touches with the make-up. "It's going great, Clay!" I exclaimed. "Come on out to the entrance way and see for yourself. It's sensational!"

Both of us walked to the arena entrance and listened to the final verse of the hymn. I saw Clay's face light up as I'd never seen it light up before. It was a new Clay Burridge who stood beside me that night, and for the first time I thought I knew — me! — what was meant by being possessed of the spirit of the Lord.

When the hymn ended the ushers began passing the offertory bags along the rows of seats. I'd expected the small orchestra to play some soft music but instead one of the guitarists picked up a violin and walked with it to centre stage. With soft orchestral accompaniment he began to play *Saving Grace*, and so help me I was never so — so touched by anything in my life. If anyone had told me, three months before when I was managing The Flack, that I'd ever be stirred by the sound of a hymn played on a fiddle I'd have known they were crazy.

When the violinist finished, the ushers brought the offertory bags to the stage, coming down the centre aisle in pairs. They handed the wooden-handled leather bags to either me or a gentleman in a business suit who whispered to me that he was Jim Stark, representing the arena. When the offertory was over Stark and I carried the bags, which were heavier than I'd ever expected them to be, back behind the stage to a small office where Fred Dunwoody, the Rev. Smoker and the arena manager were waiting. I usually stayed there, or in offices like it, until the take had been counted and the final split had been made. That night however I just had to go into the meeting and watch Clay Burridge.

Clay had made his subdued entrance and was standing behind the lectern. He had already spoken his introduction, emphasizing that the healing of the sick and the lame was not a mysterious gift given only to him, but one that could be authenticated back through history

12

to the biblical prophets. "My hand cannot even heal itself, brethren," he repeated for the fiftieth time at least since we'd been together. He quoted from memory many biblical passages from both the Old and New Testaments dealing with God's divine healing. He ended his peroration with his usual finish from the Book of Acts.

"They brought forth the sick into the streets, and laid them on beds and couches, that at least the shadow of Peter passing by might overshadow some of them. There came also a multitude out of the cities round about unto Jerusalem, bringing sick folks, and them which were vexed with unclean spirits: and they were healed every one. And the people with one accord gave heed unto those things which Philip spake . . . and many taken with palsies, and that were lame, were healed. Paul entered in, and prayed, and laid his hands on him, and healed him. So when this was done, others also, which had diseases in the island, came, and were healed."

Clay then bowed his head momentarily, and raising it said, "Will those of you who seek the healing power of the Lord Jesus Christ come forward and receive His healing grace?"

There were the usual shufflings and moving of chairs as the halt, the blind, the deaf, those on crutches and in wheelchairs, and one old lady carried on a stretcher, were brought forward by their friends or relatives down the centre aisle. Clay vaulted from the platform down to the arena floor, never looking so good since I'd met him as he did that evening, his youthful good looks and immaculate clothes, his smile that was both shy but filled with dedicated surety, his politeness and – yes tenderness, won everyone in the audience. I could *feel* it, and I felt at that moment that Clay Burridge, if he'd wanted, could have become prime minister.

The orchestra went into *Put Your Hand In The Hand*, and Clay took the hand of a little girl, then a palsied old man, followed by a woman with no outward signs of disability, murmuring a prayer over each in turn, asking them each their name, smiling down at them following his pray on their behalf, turning them away with a word of encouragement, as Paula Dunwoody turned them back to their seats. There were a great many, filling the aisle from the platform back to the rear of the arena, but unhurriedly, as if each person was the only one,

Clay spoke to them, prayed over them, and gave them an encouraging word.

The orchestra stopped playing *Put Your Hand . . .* , and the choir took over and hummed the tune of the song. Then the orchestra again. It was almost an hour before Clay finished his laying on of hands and with a deep bow to the audience walked slowly between the platform and the first row of seats and, joined by me, left the arena.

In the dressing room he shucked his suit coat, and the back of his shirt was wringing wet with sweat. I handed him a paper cup of Coca-Cola that Fred Dunwoody brought, and he sat there at the dressing table sipping it, not looking at either Fred or me.

The next day was taken over with press and radio interviews, and one of the networks phoned me from Toronto asking me to set up a TV taping of one of Clay's healing visits. I made arrangements with a motel outside of Sutton for accomodation for that night, and set up a stay in Newmarket for the two following nights. They would be much smaller meetings than the two in Peterborough, but they would give us a rest before hitting Toronto. I was to drive down to Toronto the next day to sign the contracts for the auditorium and do my advance press work.

The second night's meeting was an even greater success than the first, and dozens of people had to be turned back at the doors. After Toronto we would all be on easy street. Late that evening before leaving Peterborough we shared the money with Smoker and the other minister, and I could hardly believe the amount we'd taken in. I thanked Smoker for the great show he and his orchestra and choir had put on, and felt him out for repeat performances in the big city. That night before turning in I took a good hooker of scotch, the first drink I'd had since Quebec City.

It was almost eight o'clock when I woke up, dressed and shaved and had breakfast in the motel dining room. When I was crossing the lobby later, on the way to my room, the motel manager called to me from the desk. He was standing there with the girl desk clerk.

"Mr. Beaton, I have something for you," the manager said. He handed me an envelope and one of the motel's post cards. I shoved them in my pocket, figuring they were probably notes for Clay from a couple of admirers.

14

"Mr. Burridge has checked out," the manager said.

"Already!" Though it surprised me I thought maybe Clay had gone out for an early morning drive before we left for Sutton. He sometimes did this; to think things out he'd tell me. The desk clerk said, "He drove out of here with the car and trailer shortly after seven. Mr. and Mrs. Dunwoody were with him."

Panic hit me then, "Did he say where he was going?"

The manager said, "I think he mentioned he was going home."

"Home! Back to Nova Scotia?"

"He just said 'home,' wherever that is, Mr. Beaton. He paid the bill, including your breakfast. He said you'd understand. I've given you the receipt; it's in the envelope."

There was nothing for me to say. My agreement with Clay had just covered the percentage of the take and there was nothing in it preventing either one of us from giving up the faith-healing tour whenever we wanted to. Looking back, even before he'd mentioned it to me on the way from Perth, I realized he'd been giving a lot of thought to what he was doing, and not liking it much. As I've said, he was incorruptible, by himself or anyone else.

The desk clerk said, "He was wearing a buckskin jacket, Levis and a cowboy hat. He looked real cute."

I turned away and crossed the lobby in the direction of the inside corridor to the rooms. How could he do such a thing to me, to us? He'd just blown a fortune!

I thought of Clay Burridge driving east on the 401 freeway in his Cadillac, wearing his cowboy get-up, on his way back to Bridgewater, Nova Scotia and oblivion. A young man who'd had a million dollars in his grasp and had thrown it away.

Though I'd quit smoking a couple of months before at Clay's request, I reached into my pocket for a cigarette. My hand closed over the motel post card, which had a small piece of paper attached to it with a staple. The paper was a small newspaper clipping telling of a little girl who though suffering from diabetes had been taken off insulin by her screwball parents on the word of a faith-healer. The child had died. I guess this had been the last straw that convinced Clay he was doing wrong, though he'd never have been guilty of a thing like that. Hell, he used to *advise* some patients to seek medical help.

15

The post card bore some words printed in Clay's careful grade school style. They read: "Dear Gordon. The following verse from the book of Proverbs will explain everything. I hope 'The legs of the lame are not straight; so is a parable in the mouth of fools.' Yours in Christ. Clay."

I phoned the front desk and asked the girl to get me a taxi to take me to the bus depot.

She said, "The next bus to Toronto, if that's where you're going, Mr. Beaton, isn't until two-twenty."

I said, "Good. It'll give me time to get drunk."

WAIT UNTIL YOU'RE ASKED

We'd been standing for an hour in the queue at the Manpower Centre waiting to be interviewed for a job. Because both Bob Mansell and I, Jim Murphy, had the same last initial we were in the "M" line up. There's two things about a government bureaucracy: they're slow, and they're as impersonal as an undertaker when he sends you the final notice for his bill. Also they hire jerks as clerks.

Bob Mansell is a big guy, maybe six-four and about two hundred and ten when he's off the sauce. Me, though I'm Irish I'm small, so naturally I either take everybody's guff or get whipped for challenging guys who could eat me for breakfast. I'd met Bob ten years ago when we were working on a hydro electric dam in Northern Ontario, and since then we'd stuck pretty much together, on jobs and off. Bob had had a wife one time down in the Maritimes, but that had come to an end, and now he just played the field. I'm a bachelor, and I want to stay that way.

Anyway, on this particular morning, as I said, we were waiting to see the desk flunkie, job counsellor, or whatever the hell they call themselves. We were two weeks behind on the room rent in a flophouse bug trap on Shuter Street, which if you know Toronto at all is just about the social bottom of the ladder. The counsellor was bugging us by taking his own goddam good time slowly stirring a paper cup of coffee with one of those wooden tongue-depressors.

There was an old man ahead of Bob in the line who staggered a bit sometimes, so that Bob would take him by the shoulders and straighten him out. He'd turn to Bob and thank him, showing his toothless gums and spraying both of us with a Catawba smell, which isn't *eau de cologne*. I figured the old guy had had a few belts of cheap wine that morning, but what the hell, he was looking for a job, which is more'n you can say for most of the winos I've known.

Ahead of the old man were five or six job-seekers, and because the employment-office stiff behind the desk was a loud-mouthed show-off I could hear everything he said, as so could most of the people in the office.

There was one young guy, wearing a suit and tie, who was applying for a warehouse clerk's job that was advertised on the notice board at the back of the room.

"And what makes you think you'd make a warehouse clerk?" asked

17

the desk flunkie, looking at the young guy over the top of his counter as if he was studying something on a slide.

"I've worked at the job before."

"Oh, you have! Where?" he asked sarcastically.

"Kodak."

"Do you mean the Kodak Company of Canada?"

"Of course the Kodak Company. Where else?"

"I'll ask the questions around here. How long did you work there?"

I put the desk flunkie down right then as probably an ex-quartermaster sergeant in the Army Ordnance Corps, which is lower than shark shit.

The young man answered politely, "Five-six months."

"Were you fired?"

"No, I quit."

The desk flunkie raised his eyebrows. "Why'd you quit; was the work too tough?"

"No. Family reasons."

"What kind of family reasons?"

I could sense Bob Mansell stiffening, and I said to him, "Cool it, Bob. This jerk isn't worth it."

"In a minute I'm going to deck that son of a bitch," he said. Usually Bob is one of those quiet big guys that it takes an earthquake to arouse, but he was getting as mad as I was over the loud-mouthed questions of this smart-ass behind the counter.

The young guy answered the question about family reasons by answering, "My wife and I broke up, and I left for the West Coast to get my head together."

I knew damned well this officious clown behind the desk wasn't supposed to ask any job applicant those kind of questions, and I looked around for a sign of the manager's office so I could report him later.

The desk flunkie looked over the young guy's Social Insurance card, turned it over in his hand, then said, "This thing's illegible. What have you been doing to it?" He smiled at the other flunkies behind the counter, then at those of us standing in the queue. He was wearing what he believed was a what-would-you-do grin, but when he caught Bob Mansell's angry eye he stopped that nonsense.

18

The young guy said, "It was an accident out on the Coast. I fell into the water off a log boom. Everything in my wallet got soaked."

The desk clown handed his Social Insurance card back to him. "You'll have to get a new one," he said, dismissing him by turning to his files.

"You can still read it," the young guy said. "I been standing in line now nearly all morning! Here, I'll read you the number." He read, "Four, two, seven; three, eight, five; four, eight, nine."

"Your signature's washed out. You'll have to get a new card before I can process you."

The word "process" is one of those office-stiff words they love to use on you, as if you're a pound of sheep guts going into a mincer at a dog food company.

"Next!" the desk flunkie shouted, as if he was calling to somebody across the corner of Dundas and Jarvis instead of three feet from his desk.

The young guy walked away from the desk as if the job clerk had beaten all thoughts of him getting a job from his mind. I saw him ask a woman at another counter where to get a new Social Insurance card, and she took the card, looked it over, and handed it back to him, giving him one of those off-the-face glances and waving her hand in a general direction that *I* couldn't understand, whether the young guy could or not. She was a middle-aged drab with a pair of glasses hanging around her neck on a black velvet band; the kind of ugly bitch I've hated since public school.

The next guy stepped forward to the desk, and this time the job flunkie was all smiles. "Hello, Mr. Macdonald," he said, so that you knew *they* knew each other. The flunkie got on the phone, and within a minute got an answer. He whispered something to his friend, who nodded, and made out a job voucher without any trouble at all.

The next couple of applicants were quickly "processed," one of them getting a job on a hospital maintenance crew and the other as a counterman in a hamburger joint.

Let me say here that anybody who wants a decent job had better stay out of the Manpower Offices. The only jobs they have there are non-union joe jobs with wages at the minimum wage level.

19

When the old drunk reached the counter this civil service wart began shouting again, and smirking around at his fellow clerks. He asked, "What kind of job do you think *you* can do?"

"Almost anything that's not too heavy," the old man said.

"So you want something light, with no work attached, do you?"

The old many may have been half bombed but he was no dummy. He leaned across the counter and said in a loud voice to the desk wallah, "I'll take the kind of Mickey Mouse job *you've* got. It's light, there's no work attached, and you get your kicks making fools out of better men than you'll ever be. How'd you get this mission-stiff job anyways, delivering bills for some phony politician?"

The pen-pusher was almost apoplectic. "I'll get the police and have you arrested as a drunk. How dare you come in here in that state!"

Bob Mansell stepped forward and leaned over the desk and grabbed the flunkie by the necktie. "Don't you dare threaten this old man, you goddam scissorbill!" He pulled the flunkie half way across his desk, almost choking him with his necktie. "Now you give this old man back his Social Insurance card." The flunkie hesitated. *"Now,* you, or would you like me to open up both your ears!"

The flunkie, still held by his tie, handed the old man his card.

Bob said, "Get out of here, Pop, before the cops come. And stay the hell away from here for a while."

The old man hurried out the main door and down the stairs. The other job applicants stood back, most of them smiling happily at the sight of the desk flunkie, who'd probably given them all a hard time at one time or another, getting his.

"Now, you poor little desk dandy, I want the kind of a job you handed your friend Macdonald a few minutes ago." Still holding on to the desk flunkie he reached one of his big hands into a wire basket and pulled out the recently "processed" job invoices. He separated them on the counter top, pulling out the one made out for Macdonald. "So you gave him a job working out at Rathmore Developments, did you? At four bucks an hour. Working as a laborer and a bulldozer operator. Can he drive a bulldozer?"

"I think he can," the desk flunkie said, looking around for help.

"You *think* he can? Do you know? Eh, do you *know*, I asked you!"

"I think so."

"You think so! I've been standing there in that line-up for more than an hour listening to you getting your jollies from insulting every man who came to you for a fucking job. What do you think, we're a bunch of stiffs applying for Welfare? Eh, do you?" He put the copy of the job voucher given to Macdonald in his pocket. "Now me and my friend there want jobs with Rathmore Developments, so don't save the rest of them for *your* friends." Letting the slave trader go, he tore up a handful of vouchers and threw them on the guy's bare desk. "There, that'll give you some honest work for a change."

The flunkie took off behind the counter.

"Hey, you, what about our jobs?" I shouted after him.

"Shut up, you!" the flunkie shouted back. "Wait until you're asked, and believe me you'll wait a hell of a long time."

Bob Mansell took after him then, the two of them running along behind the counter. When he reached the end of it the employment stiff headed towards the manager's office in the corner. I got in front of him and tripped him. His glasses fell off, and I kinda accidentally crushed them under my shoe. By then he was screaming bloody murder, and several other flunkies, with more guts than brains, tried to head off Bob Mansell. He threw them off him like window dresser's dummies. Somebody, probably the manager, who had locked himself in his office, phoned the police.

When the police came they handcuffed Bob, and took us both to the station. It reminded me of the time when Bob took on a tavern full of Finns in South Porcupine.

We were lucky to get ourselves a good young Legal Aid lawyer, who got us both off with thirty days in the slammer, having the assault counts dismissed and having us charged only with creating a disturbance.

I'm writing this in the corridor of my tier at the city jail. Thirty days isn't too long a time to stay in the pokey. I'm working in the kitchen and Bob has the job of collecting the garbage cans. We've talked things over, and decided that when we get out we're heading for the Alberta tar sands, where the papers say they're going to take on four thousand men. We'll make a stake there, then go down to Edmonton and hang on the biggest binge of our lives.

I've only seen Bob Mansell real mad twice in the ten years we've been together, the time in South Porcupine and the time at the Manpower Centre. All I can say is I'm glad he's a friend of mine, for believe me I wouldn't want him as an enemy.

MOVING DAY

They had all acted real nice to him for the past week, with a shy respectfulness that he didn't even want. Eddie and his wife Laura had been up since just after daybreak, and he'd heard them talking with his grandsons, Harry and Pat, before the boys had gone off to work. Pat was studying accounting, and would be a C.A. before long, but Harry, who was handy with his hands, had gone into one of the mechanical trades, not tool-and-die making like his father and grandfather, but one of the allied trades. After the boys had left he'd heard his son and daughter-in-law whispering together in the kitchen over his bed. Of course he'd been awake much earlier than they had, thinking things over on his cot in the small basement bedroom next to the recreation room, as they called it, but which he would always think of as the cellar.

In his childhood and youth basements had always been cellars, seemingly filled with a coalbin under a window and a large ugly coal furnace with its multi-armed tin pipes tied to the beams with wire and running along the unfinished ceilings to the hot air registers in the upstairs rooms of the house. He remembered how proud his own father had been when he'd bought their first set of aluminum pipes, and how every summer they'd taken down the furnace pipes, first the tin and later the aluminum ones, to clean. He and his older brother George, and his father too, had always finished the dirty but necessary job looking like soot-dusted chimney sweeps. His mother had made them scrub up in the kitchen sink before she'd give them their supper.

It was funny too how kitchens as well as basements had changed over the years. Built-in cupboards taking the place of the old kitchen cabinets, dish-washers built-in beside the sinks, and stoves that had shrunk from the huge black monsters with their scuttle of coal and woodbox filled with kindling to small neat gas or electric stoves that brought instant heat at the turn of a dial. Thinking of the old coal stoves brought back to him the steamy smell of his woollen mitts hanging drying from the warming shelf, and of how he and George would hurry down from their upstairs bedroom to stand as close as they could to the firebox to warm themselves on winter mornings.

The mind picture he'd retained of his mother all these years was that of a housedressed mite of a woman hurrying back and forth between the stove and the kitchen table — where they always ate unless they had Sunday company such as his Aunt Edna and Uncle Jim and their kids — her thin wiry arms carrying saucepans, and plates kept warm on the stove shelf. She'd finally open the oven door, wearing the padded mitts his younger sister had sewn for her at school, and shouting happily, "Heads down!" as she maneuvered the big blue but rusty-chipped roasting pan to its place in the middle of the table, from which his father would fork the roast on to a plate and then slice it for the family. He and George would always fight for a browned slice from the outside of the roast . . .

"Dad, are you awake in there?"

It was Laura.

"Yep. I'll be upstairs in a couple of minutes."

"Do you want the usual for breakfast?"

"Yes please. Red River cereal and an egg turned over."

"And brown toast. You don't want bacon?"

"If you've got some fried, Laura."

He could hear her running up the basement stairs, and the way they boxed in the stairs today with painted wallboard and covered them with a fancy runner had seemed funny to him too. Until his wife Dorothy had died the stairs had always been left open and uncarpeted, but after Eddie and Laura and their family had moved in with him they'd changed a lot of things, mostly improvements he had to admit. Now the old cellar had become as much of a lived-in part of the house as the two upper floors. The basement rec. room, to use the term the others used, held an old green-painted upright piano and a small corner bar fronted with a pair of leather-seated bar stools. It was backed by a gilded old mirror in front of which were ranged a line of fancy but empty liqueur bottles and Italian wine bottles in their casings of straw. Eddie always kept a couple of bottles of liquor there too, one of rye and one of scotch, for the visits of friends, neighbors and guys from his job.

The furniture in the rec. room was made up of odd chairs and the old leather sofa, chair and ottoman that he and Dorothy had bought, but which had been moved downstairs from the front room when his son and daughter-in-law moved in. They'd even rigged up their old black-and-white TV set down there. "For Grandpa," he'd recently heard Laura telling her kids. His grandsons had said nothing, but his granddaughter had whined, "Jeez, Ma, what's the use of a rec. room to me if Grandpa's sleeping in his room down there?" Through the kitchen floor above his bed he'd been almost able to see the pout on her face as she said it.

Of course the child had been right. His constant presence down there had interfered with their lives long enough; it was time to get out. When he'd first mentioned moving, Ed and Laura had both opposed the idea, but he'd already made his mind up. The clincher had come on a day a couple of weeks before when he'd had a particularly bad attack, and had had to crawl up the stairs to the phone and put in an emergency call. The district fire chief had arrived, and he and his driver had given him oxygen. Then an ambulance had taken him to the hospital, where he'd spent three days in the extensive care unit. It wasn't fair to Eddie and Laura, who besides taking care of him and the house both went out to work, to impose himself on them as he'd been doing.

They'd offered to put an extension phone down into the rec. room, but he'd refused it. Then they'd protested that it was still *his* house, and his house to live in as long as he wanted. Against all their promises and protests he'd one day taken a taxi downtown and signed the property over to his son through Sam Jerome, his lawyer, and had set his affairs in order at his bank.

As he scrubbed his false teeth in the basement bathroom he thought of all the times he'd moved his presence upstairs when Harry and his fiancée were using the rec. room, or when Dina, his granddaughter, and her friend Janice had danced and fooled around down there with a long list of ever-changing boy friends, whose names he'd stopped trying to remember long before. Let's see, he thought as he fitted a new blade into his aging Gillette, Dina was now 18, born in fifty-six when he'd been department super at the plant, with young Pat born in fifty-three and Harry in fifty-one. My God, it seemed only yesterday that he and Dorothy had baby-sitted with them, a job his wife had looked forward to more than anything else he could remember. Now the three of them were old enough to get married. He mouthed an expletive and chuckled. There was still a chance he'd hold on long enough to become a great-grandfather!

"Dad!"

It was Laura again, from upstairs this time.

"I just have to finish shaving," he shouted, trying to keep the edge from his voice on this one day at least.

He shaved himself methodically and carefully, as he'd been doing for nearly sixty years, ever since he took the first fuzz off his upper lip at sixteen with his father's straight razor. He liked the feel of the warm then cooling lather on his neck and under his nose, and liked putting it on with the badger-haired, bone-handled brush Dorothy had sent him in a fully equipped toilet case during the war. A few years back one of his married daughters and her family had given him an electric shaver for Christmas, but he'd only tried it once before leaving it in his drawer until Eddie had asked him about it one day. He'd taken it up to the upstairs bathroom and left it there for his son and grandsons to use if they wanted to.

When he came out of the bathroom he noticed the small parcels on the dresser top, and figured Laura had sneaked down and put them there when he was out of the room. One of them was a carton of his brand of cigarettes and the other a fancy-wrapped packet of handkerchiefs. He put on his reading glasses and read what was printed with a pen on the paper bag holding the cigarettes. "Good luck, Gramps," it said, signed by both of Eddie's boys. Dina had placed a comic get-well card with her handkerchiefs, and beneath the humorous verse had written the promise that she'd see him soon. He took off his reading glasses, breathed on them and wiped them, then used one of the new handkerchiefs to wipe his eyes and blow his nose.

He placed the gifts, along with his old scruffed-up toilet case, in his old dried-out NAAFI suitcase that he hadn't used since — let's see? Hell, dates didn't mean anything any more! — anyway, since he and Dorothy had taken the trip in the Ford to the Gettysburg Battlefields, returning home by way of Atlantic City and Cape Cod. He and Dorothy had taken some long motor trips in those days, in a couple of earlier cars and later in the Dodge, which he'd given to young Pat to trade in on the small sports car he now drove. Let's see, the trip to Cape Cod was probably the last one they'd taken before poor Dorothy went into the hospital for the last time.

"Dad!"

It was Eddie's voice this time.

"I'm coming, I'm coming!"

"Your breakfast's getting cold."

"I'll only be a minute, Ed," he shouted from the door to his room. He heard his son close the door at the top of the basement stairs.

He crossed the rec. room to the bar, and stepping behind it picked up an unopened bottle of rye. He placed it back on the shelf, picked up an almost full bottle of scotch, filled half a tumbler with the stuff, took a bottle of lukewarm soda from beneath the bar, and filled the tumbler to the top. It was his first real drink since he'd last seen the doctor, but he *had* sneaked a few beers in the old Wanderlust Hotel near the top of the next street a couple of times. After the younger workmen had left the pub following their lunch hour the place had been left to the old men of the neighborhood, who read their newspapers or hugged their glasses of draft beer in silence. He'd looked around at them, wondering what sort of jobs they'd held or what business they'd been in, feeling that all of them, including himself, had been all reduced to the common denominator of old age.

He stared a minute at the glass in his hand, whispered, "Pipe Up Spirits, Bosun!", and downed the draft without a pause. Then he coughed and said, "Whew!"

Breakfast was still warm, despite what his son had said, but by now the scotch-and-soda was beginning to make itself felt. He pushed away half his cereal and tackled the bacon and egg on his plate. "I don't imagine they'll have my favorite cereal at the nursing home," he said. "Not that I really give a damn."

"They serve good food out at Evenlight Lodge," Eddie assured him.

"They ought to; they charge enough."

"Have you got your pills, Dad?" asked his daughter-in-law.

Without answering he pulled the small bottle of nitroglycerin capsules from his breast pocket and showed it to her.

"Is your bag packed, Dad?"

He laughed. "By Jesus, you're eager to get rid of me," he said. Then went on, "I'm ready to go to Even-Steven Lodge or whatever the hell they call it as soon as you two are ready."

27

Ed, trying not to show his surprise asked, "Dad, did you have a drink downstairs?"

"Yep. A scotch-and-soda."

Laura chided him. "Oh, Dad, you know how Dr. Duggrave warned you about smoking and drinking!"

"That young son of a bitch'll be dead before me. Anyway he told me that a drink once in a while wouldn't hurt me. What he meant of course was a half ounce of whisky mixed with a gallon of water. Never trust a teetotalling doctor. Anyhow, you've probably both heard the old saying that you meet more old drunks than you do old doctors."

Laura laughed, then said, "They'll take good care of you up at Evenlight Lodge. With rest and good food —"

"I've been getting that here, Laura, thanks to you. Their food and rest won't change things at all, and you two know it."

"You'll be under constant nursing care, Dad, and who knows, you might live to be a hundred," Ed put in.

The old man, who knew that his attacks had been increasing in frequency lately, laughed. "Yeah, and if pigs had wings, they'd make very unlikely birds, which is something *your* old grandma used to say. I figure I've been lucky to make seventy-four. Look at Jameson up the street, only fifty when he died, and all the guys I used to meet in the pub up the street on my way home from work; all gone now. And how about the Bulgarian next door but one —"

"Rumanian, Dad."

"Whatever he is. The poor old bugger lying there ever since his stroke, paralyzed all down one side, and his daughter having to feed him and everything."

Wanting to change the subject, Laura said, "When we talked to Mrs. Walker up at the lodge she told us you'd get the city papers delivered there every day."

"And I can go out for walks by myself and smoke?"

"Yes. It's in the brochure we gave you to read."

"I read it, but I believed it about as much as I used to believe the brochures from motels that your mother-in-law and I used to stay in. It seems to me that that thing is filled with more 'Don'ts' than 'Do-s.' One thing I won't quit, in my room or out of it, is smoking." He lit up a cigarette. "I've a good mind not to go out to that nuthouse after all," he added teasingly. "Maybe I'll just flake out for good right here. I read somewhere that with a fatal massive heart attack you just drop in your tracks. No mess or trouble at all."

His son and daughter-in-law exchanged quick glances.

The old man laughed to show them he'd been only joking. "Thank young Dina and the boys for their presents," he said: "You two are lucky to have had kids like them. Of course, Eddie, your mother and I were lucky too." Then he quickly added, "And that goes for your parents too, Laura."

Laura said, "The boys went to work before you got up, and Dina slept at Janice's place last night."

"I heard both boys leave; I've been awake since four o'clock. I should have taken a bash of that scotch then. By God I haven't felt better since I first saw that quack Duggrave. By the way, that's a hell of a name for a doctor. Besides I think he's a Holy Roller or something. It seems to me he's always saying, 'Cut out smoking and drinking and you're not only sure to go to heaven, but even later than if you don't cut them out.' "

Laura went upstairs to get ready.

As soon as she was gone the old man said, "Now get me another scotch, Eddie. A good one, full tumbler, half liquor and half soda."

Laura returned to the kitchen wearing a new dress and shoes.

"You look real pretty, Laura," her father-in-law said. "as if you're going to a wedding instead of a wake."

"Dad!"

The old man said, "Maybe I was crazy to agree to go to this nursing home, but I won't back out now that I've put you two to all the trouble of getting me in. I'm not senile yet, so I'm not being committed, and I can leave the joint anytime, right?"

"Sure you can, Dad. But Evenlight is a great —"

"That's some name, Evenlight. Ever hear of an uneven light? Get me that drink, Eddie, and not the five-to-one soda to whiskey drink you pour for those teetotalling friends of yours."

Ed went down to the bar.

Laura said, "They have a nice big back lawn, some of it planted in small personal flower gardens by the guests –"

"Funny how places like that change the word 'patient' to 'guest,' isn't it?"

"–And a local service club up there takes the guests on car tours –"

"Oh Christ! I don't want a bunch of hick-town dentists, garage owners and real estate crooks taking me out to show me the goddam autumn leaves. Too bad they can't take the expense off their income tax."

"They have bingo once a week."

"I can just see myself playing bingo with a bunch of old biddies who've already reached their dotage. Why, I used to refuse to go to bingo games with your mother-in-law when she was alive." Adding sorrowfully, "She loved bingo too. I wish now for her sake I'd have gone with her."

Laura said, "They call it Evenlight, you know, like Evening Light or something."

Surprisingly the old man said, *"And as the evening twilight fades away, The sky is filled with stars, invisible by day."* Adding, "That's Longfellow."

Laura stared at him open-mouthed.

Trying to cover up a side of him he'd never shown before, the old man shouted in the direction of the basement stairs, "Hey, waiter, where's my drink!"

Before walking down to Eddie's car the old man stood on the concrete porch and looked at a spot near his feet. Imprinted there was the petite print of a woman's slippered foot. "That's your mother's real gravestone to me," he said to his son. "Not that overpriced piece of granite up in Mount Hope. Don't ever cement it over. I remember the morning after the porch floor had been poured, and she came out to pick up the paper, forgetting the concrete hadn't had time to dry."

He refused any help going down the steps to the front walk, but when he reached the car he stood on the sidewalk and took a long look at the house. "I hope you two and your family are as happy in it as we were. Thanks to you, Eddie, it's a lot better looking now than it was the day in 1948 when we moved in. Do you still remember when we moved out of the old rented house in Riverdale? I didn't say much about it then to you kids, but there were times when eighty-nine hundred dollars seemed like a fortune. Anyhow she's long been paid for, and I wouldn't want to even hear what it's worth at today's prices."

He turned to Eddie and asked, grinning, "Remember the summer when you and I tore down the old veranda, and I had Gus Romasca and his boy come over with their small concrete mixer, and between us we built the new front porch? That second step is still off level a quarter of an inch at its south end. Funny how that's always bugged me; my precision tool training I guess."

"I remember us building it, Dad."

"Funny the things you remember, isn't it? Your mother nattered at us for a week for tramping sand into the house." He laughed.

Looking across the street he spotted old lady Williser peering from between her drapes. "Look at that old nosey bitch!" he exclaimed, pointing. "Spent her whole jeezly lifetime keeping kids off her lawn. There's another that's gone, Barney Williser. Cirrhosis of the liver in 1971. And that wife of his drove him to his death."

He climbed into the back seat, and Ed could see him staring through the back window until the car turned the corner on to the crosstown street.

A couple of minutes later he said, "Well, there goes the old Wanderlust Hotel. I'll bet I spent thousands of bucks on their beer over the years. Your mother and I used to drop in after the early movie at the Woodcrest picture show, and I spent many a Saturday afternoon there while she did her weekly shopping. To say nothing of the beers I'd drink there after work. The old Woodcrest is now a credit furniture store, isn't it?"

"Yep. Like a lot of neighborhood movie houses it closed up in the mid-fifties when TV came in."

"You know, the last time I was in the old pub I didn't know a soul there any more. Since Bobby Arbuthnot's heirs sold the place I don't even know any of the waiters any more."

"Did you ever go down to the Legion Hall, Dad?"

"Not since just after the war, when the beer in the pubs was rationed and they used to close down early. I never belonged to it, and haven't been inside a Legion Hall for years."

As they sped north towards the small town where Evenlight Lodge was located, the old man sat quietly drunk in the back seat of the car. They passed a small sign at a sideroad with an Arrow pointing along it and bearing the word Rabbittown.

"Rabbittown," the old man said. "I'll bet neither one of you ever met anybody from there, did you?"

Ed said, "No, Dad, I never did."

Laura shook her head.

"Well *I* did," the old man said. "A stoker P.O. in the navy. Name of Keater. That was when I was Chief E.R.A. on the *Port Credit*."

As if she'd been counting back over the years, Laura spoke over her shoulder, "You know, Dad, you were pretty old to join the navy when you did."

The old man laughed. "I had a couple of captains who were older than me, and some of those old buggers who volunteered in the Royal Navy to be convoy commodores were as old as I am now. They used to run the convoy from the bridge of a merchant ship or a tanker, and I'll bet plenty of them got it. They must have been great old guys."

"How old were you when you joined up in '39?"

"Thirty-seven, which was fairly old compared with most of the kids on the ships. I was forty-four when I got out. How old were *you* then, Eddie?"

"In forty-five, let's see, eighteen I guess."

"You two'll be grandparents yourselves before you know it. Funny how things go, isn't it?"

Laura said, "It's a toss up who gets married first, Harry or Dina."

The old man laughed. "By the time I'm a great grandfather I'll just be another paid-up entry in some undertaker's ledger." Then he said, "Funny how I should remember Keater, and that he came from Rabbittown. He was ten years younger'n me so I guess he's still alive somewhere, maybe he still lives in Rabbittown."

Laura turned around in her seat and asked, "How come you joined up in 1939 at the age of thirty-seven, Dad? As a tool-and-die maker you could have got a deferment couldn't you?"

"Yeh, they were short of them. I don't know why exactly; maybe I didn't want to stay behind with the scissorbills. The navy was already planning to build the corvettes I guess, and they found they couldn't recruit enough trained ship's engineers. What they did was take guys like me from the mechanical trades and make us over into petty officer engine room artificers. Being a journeyman tool-and-die maker I qualified, so I enlisted." He laughed. "Hell, we had hoisting engineers from the northern mining towns, guys who repaired and ran the machinery in prairie grain elevators, locomotive mechanics from the C.N. shops in Stratford, all kinds of men with machine training. Somehow they taught us how to run, and repair at sea if necessary, oil-fired steam reciprocating engines."

"That's the first time I ever heard you talk about the war."

"Nothing much to talk about. During action I was always in the engineroom. I just had to guess at what was going on up top."

The old man was asleep by the time they pulled up in front of Evenlight Lodge.

"Dad, we're here," Laura said.

The old man woke up, wiped his glasses on his new handkerchief, and gazed through the car window at the large Victorian frame house with its two-story red brick side and back additions. There were a couple of cars parked in the circling driveway, and three old men, one wearing a straw hat and the other a peaked cap, sitting on pieces of lawn furniture, each separating himself from the others. An old woman with a six-quart fruit basket on the ground beside her was trimming a flower bed on the edge of the lawn.

"Well?" asked Laura.

"We'll see," answered her father-in-law.

"You'll make friends with some of the men your own age, Dad," his son said. "Evenlight has an excellent reputation. We visited a half dozen places before we chose it."

The old man laughed. "It's a cinch I'm not going to be too friendly with those zombies sitting there on the lawn. I hope they have some patients who still have their marbles." He laughed again and asked, "Who gives a place like this its reputation, the local undertaker?" He lit a cigarette and said, "Don't worry, I can make myself at home anywhere."

"The main thing is, Dad, that you'll be under constant medical care here," Ed said.

"Yeah I know."

Before getting out of the car he told his son and his wife, "Sam Jerome, my lawyer, has my papers and things, including my spare safety deposit key sealed in an envelope. My will and some bonds are in my safety deposit box. I wrote out all my instructions the other day; they're under some clothes in the second drawer of my dresser. Sam will be paying the rent, fees, or whatever they call them here. My pension cheques will be going to him too."

"Of course, Dad," Laura said.

"I think Dina should have my old basement bedroom; that gives the boys separate rooms upstairs."

The couple in the front seat both nodded.

"If you should hear of me leaving here, don't go into a panic. I'm still a free citizen, and there's nothing wrong with my head. I won't be moving back into your house again--"

"But you'll let us take you down to the city for visits, won't you?"

"Visits sure. If I hang on long enough I'd like to attend at least one of my grandchildren's weddings."

"I'll arrange it for sure, Dad," Ed said.

"But don't push any of them into marriage on my account." The old man opened the car door. "Now, Eddie, get my old NAAFI bag out of the trunk for me, will you? I'll leave you two here."

Laura took a small gift-wrapped package from her purse and handed it over the back of the seat. "Here, Dad. It's just a small memento from me to thank you for everything you've done for us."

"Thank you very much, Laura. May I peek at it?"

"Sure."

With palsied hands the old man tore off the wrappings and opened the box they'd contained. Inside the box was a small leather traveling clock. "This is very nice of you, and thoughtful of you too, Laura."

"It's got an alarm."

The old man laughed. "I've got my own built-in alarms these days,"

34

he said. He leaned forward and kissed his daughter-in-law.

After getting out of the car he took his suitcase from his son.

"I'll carry it into the lodge for you, Dad."

"I'll carry it myself, Eddie, and check myself in too." He pressed his son's hand. "I've always been proud of you, Eddie, and your sisters too." Turning to the open window of the car he said, "Ed couldn't have married a better wife, Laura. Now both of you take good care of the kids."

They watched the old man, not too steady in his walk while carrying the heavy bag, climb the couple of steps to the screened front door of the house. At the last minute, after putting down the bag and opening the screen door, he turned, smiled and waved at them, his wave both a gesture of goodbye and one telling them to leave.

After turning the car around and leaving Evenlight Lodge behind, Ed said, "He was trying to act tough. Both for our sakes and to make out it didn't matter. He always was a tough old guy. And independent. Jeez, I never knew a man so independent."

Laura nodded into her handkerchief.

"What else can I say about him except that he was a very good father and a decent man."

"That's all he ever expected anyone to say. Anything else would only have embarrassed him or made him laugh."

Ed said, "Dr. Duggrave only gives him a few more months at most, you know."

"I know." Laura began sobbing into her handkerchief.

They were silent for the next few miles, but then Laura asked, "Do you think your father really wanted to move out of the house, Ed?"

"No. I really think we're to blame for sending him away, Laura. All of us, me, you, and the kids. In the old days families didn't send the grandparents to nursing homes; they stayed in the house with their families until they died. Today we're like aboriginal Eskimos, without the Eskimo's economic reasons for leaving the elderly in a snowdrift to die."

"Yes," Laura said, beginning to weep again.

The old man placed his heavy bag on the floor just inside the screen door. Then he took a couple of nitroglycerin pills from the bottle in his pocket and popped them under his tongue. He sat down on a chair waiting for the pain in his chest and upper left arm to ease a bit. He looked around for an ash tray, and seeing none threw his cigarette butt outside after shoving open the screen door.

When he pressed the small desk bell on a small hall table a middle-aged woman with blue-grey hair and an officiousness that she tried to conceal with a pressed-lip smile came out of an office and gave him a questioning look.

"My name is Alex Benson," he said. "My son, Ed Benson, or his wife Laura, made arrangements for me to be admitted here I believe."

"You came here alone?" she asked him, looking down with a faint distaste at his leather-cornered green canvas NAAFI suitcase.

"No, my son and daughter-in-law drove me up here. I asked them to leave. Are you Mrs. Walker?"

"Yes." She led the way to the office doorway, and the old man sat down in a chair across the desk from her.

As she took a file folder from a desk drawer she said, "I'm sure you'll feel at home here at Evenlight, Mr. Benson."

"I'll try," he answered. "Things seem awfully quiet around here though."

She smiled, and he noticed that her smile was still that of the bureaucratic clerk.

He glanced at the doorway. "Where is everybody, Mrs. Walker?"

"Some of our guests are out shopping on the main street, and two or three of the men are fishing above the dam in the river behind the lodge." She scanned his file. "I see you're a medical guest, Mr. Benson, but no one seems to have signed you in."

"I told them not to; I'll do *that* myself."

"That's — that's not usually done here, sir."

The old man stood up. "Okay, call me a cab, and I'll go over to the highway or bus depot or somewhere and get out."

"Please sit down, Mr. Benson," the woman said. She handed him his admittance sheet and he signed it.

"Now I've signed myself in, I will also sign myself out whenever I want to," he said.

She seemed flustered by the turn of events, but she immediately caught herself and became once again the efficient bureaucrat. "Medical guests, and those who have been placed in here for safekeeping by relatives, unlike the very few who suffer from slight mental problems, may go into town during the prescribed hours unaccompanied," she said.

"I won't be accompanied anywhere," he said.

She smiled a difficult and twisted smile as she replied, "As I said, Mr. Benson, you're a medical guest."

"How far is the main street from here?"

"Just around the bend in the road beyond the lodge; actually we are *on* the main street now, Suffolk Avenue, and there is only a short bridge to cross to reach the stores."

"I see. Has the town got a bar or a pub?"

She chewed a moment on her words before answering him. "Yes. We don't mind our guests dropping into the Suffolk House for a beer on occasion, but we don't tolerate intoxication." She gave him her institutional smile and said, "I'm sure, Mr. Benson, we wouldn't do that, would we?"

He said to himself, Speak for yourself, lady.

She handed him a Xeroxed sheet, which he folded and shoved into his pocket.

"Those instructions contain the exact times meals are served, and our guests are expected to adhere to them faithfully. There are also a few lodge regulations, times of visiting hours, etcetera, Mr. Benson. Dr. Dengast, our physician, will be along this afternoon. He makes a regular weekly call but is always close at hand by telephone at any time. I suppose he'll want to examine you."

"Are there nurses here?"

"Yes. We have a registered nurse on every staff shift."

With Mrs. Walker carrying his bag and leading the way along the main floor corridor they entered what he took to be the new brick section of the building. She opened a door and said, "Here's your own room, Mr. Benson. Just make yourself at home."

The room contained a built-in closet, bed, dresser and easy chair.

Actually it was quite pleasant.

"Mrs. Walker, I don't see an ash tray," he said.

"You smoke, Mr. Benson?"

"I've been smoking for sixty years, Mrs. Walker, and I'm not quitting now. I read your brochure, and asked my son and his wife about it, and there was no regulation about being unable to smoke in my room."

Without a word the woman left the room, returning in a couple of minutes with a five-and-ten store ash tray. "Please be careful," she said. He noticed she no longer used his name as a suffix to her sentences.

"Don't worry, I've been smoking in my own house most of my life without setting fire to it. And I don't smoke in bed."

"Well that's — that's reassuring."

"Where is the bathroom, please?"

"Right next door to our left. We're lucky to have it so handy, aren't we?"

He grinned at her use of the pronoun "we." As if she sensed the reason behind his grin she hurried out of the room, shutting the door behind her.

He checked inside a slit in the lining of his suitcase to make sure his bank courtesy card and cheque book were there, then hung his jacket in the closet.

His window looked out on a large grassed backyard, part of which was laid out in miniature flower gardens. There was nobody to be seen.

He removed his shoes and lay down on top of the bed. He stared up at the clinically white ceiling, hating the place already and wondering if it was here, between the four bare olive-green walls, that he was destined to finally pack it in. It was only then, in a loneliness and despair he'd hidden up to now, that he began to cry.

SEE YOU IN SEPTEMBER

The young girl in the *Hostesses de Paris* booth at the Gare de Lyon had told him with professional disinterest that Judy's hotel was not in Montparnasse as he had thought but in St. Germain des Pres. She had pointed out the location on a city map, marked it with an inked cross, and handed it over the counter to him.

"*Bienvenue á Paris, M'sieur*," she repeated by rote.

"*Merci bien*. Thank you," he'd said in return, glad to switch back to English. "Would you call the Hotel Scribe and confirm my reservation there please?"

"Certainly. Your name, sir?" More respectfully now.

"Michael Hammond."

The girl returned to her desk and spoke to somebody over the phone. All he was able to catch was his name, "M'sieu Ham-mond." There was more French that he couldn't understand then the girl asked him, "From where do you come, sir?"

"Canada," he answered.

"But this morning please?"

"Oh, Rome. Before that *Le Festival du Cinema* in Cannes."

After some more rapid French she turned and said, "Your room is reserved, sir, at *l'Hotel Scribe*."

"Good. Thank you. *Merci*."

He slung his Air France bag on his shoulder, picked up his suitcase and attache case and walked out of the station to a line of cabs.

His driver, a young hippie with his long unkempt hair caught up in a khaki beret, drove across the Seine, though Hammond knew very well that his hotel was not on the Left Bank. They sped recklessly along the various quays through the Latin Quarter while Hammond glanced cursorily at the groups of young people they passed.

"*L'etudiants!*" the driver cursed when he caught his passenger watching them through the window. "*Tout Maoists!*"

"*Je ne parle pas Francais*," Hammond said.

"*Allemande?*"

"No. *Anglais*."

"Yeah! Speak me a leetle Eenglish," the driver said, turning a gap-toothed grin to his passenger and just missing a bicycle rider with a ten-foot ladder on his shoulder.

Hammond ignored the driver from then on, wondering once again after nine months of wondering, why Judy had insisted on coming to the Sorbonne for her degree. What the hell was the title of her thesis? The Dioptric Allusions of Cartesian Methodology in Rationalist Philosphy. It had taken him a week at home to memorize it, fantasizing on a nude Judy sitting at the foot of his bed as he did so. A fantasy dualism of esoteric scholarship and *Playboy* centrefold.

When a pair of jeans-clad girls with long straight hair strolled in front of the cab, bringing it to a bolt-loosening stop, the driver's scatalogical screams put Judy out of his mind for a moment. The girls halted in the middle of the street and with smiling casualness each gave the cabby a symbolic thrust with their middle finger.

The cab-driver, silenced from then on by choleric anger, finally deposited Hammond at his hotel, where he was given his fare and a precise 15 percent tip.

It was late in the afternoon when his phone rang and Judy's happy but somehow huskier voice said, "Mike, I just got in."

"Hi, Judy."

"What's this I'm calling, The Ritz?"

He laughed. "No. The Scribe."

"I knew it was somewhere over there among the fat cats. Have you just come up from the Festival?"

"I was in Rome for a few days. I arrived by train this morning."

"It's good to hear your voice, Mike. How long're you hanging around my new home town?"

"A couple of days at least, maybe longer. Hasn't school packed up yet?"

"Not for me. I'm having my thesis typed and bound by a Polish-Jewish girl who speaks every European language but English."

"The Dioptric Allusions of − "

Together they finished, " − Cartesian Methodology in Rationalist Philosophy." Then Judy exclaimed, "You remembered it!"

"It only took a week to memorize."

She laughed and asked, "When do you want to see me?"

"Now."

"No, seriously, Mike."

40

"As soon as I can. I've been sitting here since noon, except for a short trip around the corner to the Cafe de la Paix for a double cognac."

Her husky laugh came through the phone as she said, "You fool, Mike. Don't you know that drinks around the Opera are double the price anywhere else?"

"As a movie producer I thought I'd treat myself."

"How did *The Fireflies* go at the Festival, Mike?"

"Lousy, of course. I was told it was panned by every critic but the one from *L'Osservatore Romano*."

"The Vatican paper!"

"It that's what it is. It's Italian anyway."

"Poor Mike!"

"Nothing ventured, nothing gained. Even if my venturing was really using my father's money."

Judy asked him how the members of both their families were doing, and he told her he'd talked to her mother on the phone before leaving home.

"What was Mom doing, collecting used brassieres for the starving Biafrans — no, that was a few years ago — the Bengali refugees?"

He laughed. "She's been elected Chairwoman of the club's anti-abortionist league or something."

"The menopausal Mafia," Judy said soberly. Then cheering up again she said, "Come over to my side of town and pick me up in an hour for dinner."

"Okay. In the meantime I'll have another cognac to make me forget the Film Festival."

"I'm really sorry about that, Mike."

"It taught Wilson and me what not to do in our next picture."

"Is he here in Paris with you?"

"No. Jerry fell in love with a Swedish girl from Malmö, and they took off for Venice and Florence together."

"I'm glad."

"So am I, Judy. I wanted there to be just us." He hesitated before asking, "You *do* live alone, don't you?"

"Most of the time, except for Peter Pumpkin."

41

"Who's that!"

"My linnet. You've heard the Cockney song, *With my old cock linnet*. Dum-de-da-da. Peter's a little green bird in a cage, except he's colored almost yellow. That's where his last name of Pumpkin comes in."

"You're crazy, Judy."

"Not quite — yet. You ever live with old René Descartes philosophy for nine months?"

"Judy, you haven't changed a bit," he said, laughing.

"Neither have you, from what you've told me so far. Go out and have your brandy and watch out for young ladies in mini skirts wearing large onyx rings on both hands and carrying heavy weighted handbags. Their prices are away up due to the inflation."

"I've been avoiding them. *I thought it was my masculine charm.*"

"*It was your masculine* money, dearie. You know where I am, next door to the Brasserie Lipp on the Boulevard St. Germain." She hung up without warning as she'd always done.

The Grand Hotel Taranne was lost between two sidewalk cafes, one belonging to the Brasserie Lipp and the other to a small cafe on its other flank. It was a narrow six-story building two rooms wide by the look of it. He traversed the narrow foyer and enquired of a woman in a back office, "Miss Craig, *sil vous plait*?"

"Cra-ig? Judy? *Chambre cinquante deux, M'sieur*."

"*Merci, Madam*."

As the tiny elevator carried him slowly to the fifth floor he tried to bring his relationship with Judy back into focus. Their families had been summer neighbors when they were children, though Judy was six years younger than he. That would make her twenty-four now. The last time he'd seen her was more than a year before up at Windermere, where the Hammond and Craig clans had summered since their grandfathers' time. She'd been withdrawn and sullen and given to taking lone trips around the lake in one of the speedboats. The only time she'd come out of her shell with him was at a Saturday night dance at the hotel when she'd told him she was coming to Paris to get her degree. They were sitting together on a veranda swing.

"A degree in what, Judy?"

"Cartesian philosophy."

"Why not get it down in the city?"

"Oh, a couple of reasons." She had thrown her arms wide to encompass much more than the resort hotel and its cottages, much more even than the Muskoka lake, her flung-out arms covering Toronto and her past, and even her family. "I want to get away from this – this crap," she'd said.

"But why the Sorbonne?"

"Because old Descartes was a Frenchman. If I was an anthropologist studying the Micronesians would you expect me to study them at U of T or York?"

He'd laughed. "I guess not." Then, "Why Descartes?"

"I dunno. I met him in a physics class at Bishop Strachan when we were playing around with light refraction, and later I read up on him. I was interested in a philospher who also knew a lot about lenses."

"Judy, you amaze me. You really do."

"So long as I don't scare you. Do you want to come for a boat ride to my secret hideaway, Mike?"

"Okay."

"I'll fix it up with Turner down at the boathouse while you steal a bottle of liquor from the bar," she'd said, taking off her shoes and bounding down the veranda steps. By the time he'd reached the boathouse with a bottle of whiskey she was sitting at the wheel of a small powerboat, and as soon as he stepped in they shot away from the dock. Far down the lake Judy pulled into a small decrepit wharf and jumping ashore said to him, "Welcome to Craig Beach."

"It even has your name on it?" he asked grinning.

"My grandad's; he planted these trees before he went off to die for King and Country in 1914."

They'd sat on the soft prickly bed of pine needles beneath the tall white pines, after Judy had dumped some of the whiskey into the ground and filled its void with cold lake water. She'd taken a long gulp of it and after he'd followed her example he'd found the impromptu mix was somehow just right.

Some time later, after she'd seduced him and they were both lying nude and half drunk on the pine needles, he'd said, "Judy, I should come to Paris with you."

"No. In the first place, Mike, you don't speak French, and I'm leaving *everything* behind, remember?"

"From now on I'm going to miss you."

"That's sweet. Incidentally, what are *you* going to do?"

"Maybe make a movie. Jerry Wilson has a film script he wants to direct, and he'd like me to produce it."

"What does Colonel Hammond think of that?"

"I think my father's glad I'm going to something creative."

"Yeah, creative like in 'creative advertising,' she'd said, throwing the empty bottle over her head into the grove of trees. She stood up then and pulled on her clothes, motioning him to do the same.

He'd tried to kiss her in the boat and again when they tied it up at the boathouse, but she turned her head aside and gently pushed him away. Though he'd called her at her house in the city several times she'd refused to answer the phone. Then he'd heard she'd left for Paris.

When the elevator stopped at the fifth floor he crossed the narrow space to No. 52 and knocked on the door.

"Be right with you," said Judy's voice from inside the room.

In a moment she opened the door and stood there wearing a soiled pink terrycloth robe. She was without make-up and her brown hair was damp and hanging carelessly. Her face and the hands that gripped his own were much thinner than he remembered them. She pulled him into the room and sat him down on the single bed.

"I've just come out of the shower?" she said as she gathered up a pair of blue denim jeans, a boy's blue workshirt and a green cardigan sweater of uncertain gender and carried them into the bathroom. The room was cheaply and sparsely furnished and there was an old unpainted womans' bicycle propped against the closet doors. A small green-and-yellow bird the size of a canary stared at him with a doleful eye from its cage on the windowsill.

He walked to the window and stared over the cage into the heavy traffic of the boulevard, and across it at the two cafés, the Flore, and the Deux Magots at the corner across from the church.

When he turned around he found Judy, minus a brassiere, pulling on her jeans in the bathroom doorway. He took a step in her direction but she motioned him away. "In the top drawer of the dresser you'll find a blue-and-white striped blouse. Hand it to me, will you?"

She removed its laundry tag and undid its top buttons before pulling it over her head. Then kneeling on the floor she pulled a pair of cork-soled slip-ons from beneath the dresser and adjusted the straps around her heels. She disappeared once more into the bathroom, where he could hear her cursing in French and English as she combed the snarls from her hair. When she came out once more she looked kookily charming.

"You know, Judy, you're still a knockout."

With her husky laugh she said, "It's what all us Cartesian philosophers are wearing this season." She reached into an oversize leather bag and pulled out a pack of Gauloise cigarettes, offering him one.

He shook his head. "I kicked the habit last winter."

Blowing a cloud of smoke towards the ceiling she said, "You don't get lung cancer from *Les Bleus*. They kill you quicker than that. Trench mouth or something." She took the birdcage from the windowsill and placed it on the dresser. Staring down into the wide boulevard she asked, "How do you like my neighborhood, Mike?"

"It's hectic during rush hour."

"It's hectic most of the time. Right down here below the hotel there was a pitched battle between the riot flics and the revolutionary students back in sixty-eight. I'll show you a machine-gun bullet still lodged in the wall above the front door. Madam Mortier, the owner here — she laughs when I call her 'Mrs. Cement' — says that again in 1970, when they were putting in a new entrance to the Metro station, some of the Maoists set fire to the boulevard with a drum of gasoline and rolled-up newspaper torches."

He circled her with his arm, his hand flat against her hip. "Who are the Maoists?"

"It's a generic term here for anyone who is to the left of the old line Communist Party, especially students."

"My cab driver used the word this morning."

"What was the little fascist's name, Jean Genet?" Then, as if she'd been convinced he wouldn't know what she was talking about she went on, "Across the road the Café Flore was the former hangout of Simone de Beauvoir and Jean-Paul Sartre."

He didn't know who they were.

She straightened up and he let his hand slide across her buttocks.

"Let's go and eat, Mike," she said, picking up her bag and shooing him out of the room. In the small elevator she let him cup his hands over her unfettered breasts, releasing herself before they reached the street floor.

On the sidewalk he asked, "Do you want to eat here at the Brasserie Lipp? I understand it has Guide Michelin stars."

"No, Mike. The Lipp is now the once-a-week eating spot for James Jones who lives over on one of the islands in the river. You know Jones; the guy who wrote *From Here To Eternity*?"

"Yeah! Really?" Mike stared at the restaurant as they passed it.

"Where do you want to go then?"

She took his hand as they passed a tiny cinema, and led him upstairs in Le Drugstore on the corner, where they found an empty booth against a window overlooking the square. When the waitress came, Judy ordered them each a ham-and-cabbage salad and a large bottle of Beaujolais '69. "Their salads are the best in Paris," she told him.

When the young waitress served them their orders and the wine, Mike was surprised to find that the salads filled large earthenware bowls, the cabbage and ham sliced in paper-thin strips. After adding the homemade dressing they both ate hungrily and without speaking. It wasn't until Mike had wiped his mouth with his napkin and refilled their wine glasses that he broke the silence. "Absolutely the best salad I've ever eaten," he said.

"Do you want anything else?" she asked.

"No. There's no room left. How about you?"

She shook her head as she finished her wine and refilled their glasses again, emptying the bottle. Then she said, "I want to show you my neighborhood before dark."

When they descended from the restaurant Mike found himself being led along a narrow curving corridor lined with tiny boutiques. They came up into a side street with a sign reading Rue de Rennes. Ahead of them, squatting in the doorway of a small darkened department store, were a pair of genuine Parisian *clochards*, an old man and woman, as filthy a pair of human beings as Mike had ever not wanted to see. The man, whose face was covered with a once-grey beard like that of a dirty Santa Claus, and his partner who was dressed in something that reminded him of a grubby patchwork quilt, sang out before they reached them, "'ello, Judy!"

"*'ello, mon vieux*," Judy said.

From somewhere she took a small handful of coins and pressed them into the old male tramp's hand, before taking Mike's arm and leading him across the street.

"You know those — people?" he asked.

"Sure. They're my mascots, Heléne and Claude. You'd never guess it now but Claude was a famous hero in the *Resistance*. In the winter they sleep on the warm subway grating over the St. Germain des Pres Metro station." She pointed down a narrower sidestreet. "That's where I do most of my shopping, and my laundry." She pinched one of the short sleeves of her blouse. "Dress-up clothes like this I have washed and ironed by Renée at the *Automatique*, but the rest I do myself."

They continued along St. Germain to St. Michel and down it past stores, office buildings, a bank and some stone university buildings until she led him along a smaller street where most of the Sorbonne buildings were built of brick. Judy pulled him to a halt and pointed at one of the buildings. "That's where I go to school," she said.

"It's not very impressive, is it?" he asked. "To me it looks like a boxboard factory."

There was an edge now to her laugh as she turned him around and led him back to the Boul Mich. "We can take a walk through the Luxembourg Gardens if they haven't locked the gates yet," she said. The edge on her laugh had now transferred itself to the words she spoke.

They crossed the wide boulevard and entered the gardens, walking halfway through them before finding an empty park bench in front of the Palais.

"Why don't you come back home with me, Judy?" Mike asked.

She was long in answering him. "Several reasons I guess. I haven't submitted my thesis yet for one thing, and if and when I *do* go back to Canada I'm not going back to Forest Hill"

"That's crazy, Judy!"

"No, Mike, it's free will. I guess you didn't bother to find out from any of the Craig clan — though you did talk to my mother — that I've been cut off from the family hoard of profitable real estate and blue chip coupon-clipping."

47

He stared at her. "No, I didn't know that Judy." Then smiling he added, "I'm sure your parents would welcome you back, dear." He took one of her hands in his.

"I'm sure they would, Mike," she said, flashing a wry smile. "Mother would give her right arm to have me marry into what she still thinks of as her own class." She gave a short mocking laugh. "She'd love to put on a white wedding for her daughter at Timothy Eaton Memorial Church and a reception later at the Granite Club. She'd even talk Dad into buying my acceptable husband and me a nice house on the Bridle Path or the correct side of Bayview Avenue."

"What's wrong with that?" he asked.

She faced him, and taking her hand from his patted the back of his own. "You're a square, Mike, a real upwardly mobile square. The world has changed since we were kids up at Windermere ten, twenty years and you haven't even noticed it. Your particular values lost their identity following World War Two, and especially in the youth revolution of the sixties, but you'd long been insulated against such changes. Poor Mike."

She placed her arms along the back of the bench and stared across the path at some small children playing on the grass.

He kicked some gravel, watching the dust settle on his highly polished hand-sewn loafers. "How are you supporting yourself, Judy?" he asked without raising his head.

"I get along. It doesn't take much money to live at the Taranne on a permanent basis. Madam Mortier makes her money out of the tourists."

"It still costs *some* money," he said, accusingly, turning to face her.

She nodded and said, "But all the guesses that are making you uptight are wrong ones. I think I'm still pretty, and no pretty girl ever starved to death in Paris."

"Have you a lover?" he asked, his voice quivering.

She didn't answer him, but continued to watch the playing children. "Let me take you home with me. This city is the European equivalent of – of Hollywood or Las Vegas."

"Mainly for French, Belgian and Swiss girls," she said. "Thanks though for your offer."

48

"When do you intend to come home then?"

"September."

"And you intend to continue living as you do, whatever way that is, until then?"

"I hope to. With perhaps a holiday trip to the Normandy coast during August. Everyone leaves Paris during August."

He stood up, changed his mind, and sat down again.

With her eyes still on the playing children she said, "As you told me earlier, Mike, it's your father's money you're using on your ego trip as a *nouveau vague* picture producer. I haven't been quite honest with you; I read a sarcastic review of *The Fireflies* in a small radical film magazine last week. Among the more kindlier things the reviewer said was that the film was amateurish and incompetent. Your retarded – no, sorry – your atavistic, and that's the wrong word too – point of view is no longer a saleable commodity to a film audience. *La haute* as dramatic types have ceased to exist."

"Now you're a film critic too!" he said, bitterly angry. "You'd sooner take the rantings of some Commie critic than believe in me."

"That's unfair. I was hoping perhaps as much as you were that the film would be a success. That it would make a creative and artistic success of you too."

Their argument was broken by the arrival of two boys wearing Levis, one of them in a U.S. college sweatshirt and the other wearing a dirty torn sweater. The sweatshirted one poured out a torrent of rapid French at Mike, who turned desperately to Judy.

She told him, "These boys are attending summer classes over at the university. They would like you to give them a few francs with which they could get something to eat."

"You American, Mac?" the boy asked Mike through the smile that had appeared on his face at the sound of Judy's English.

"No, I'm a Canadian," Mike answered dryly.

"I'm American," the boy said. Then, as if the ties of a fading British Empire might do the trick, he went on. "My buddy there's an Australian." Turning, he shouted, "Hey, Cobber, come over here. This gentleman's a Canadian."

The other boy joined his friend, and in his Cockney-sounding accent explained that they were temporarily broke until the end of the month, and they'd appreciate a little change to buy something to eat.

Mike said, "No. Sorry."

Despite their disappointment at the turn-down the American boy said, "Okay, Mac, sorry to have bothered you." They both turned to leave.

"Just a minute, you guys," Judy said, groping deep in the contents of her oversized handbag. She came up with one folded piece of French paper money which she handed to the American boy.

"Thanks very much," he said.

"Thank you, Miss," his Australian buddy added before they walked away. Neither of them even looked at Mike.

Judy stood up. "Let's go," she said. "They'll soon be clearing everyone out of the gardens."

They walked in silence through the Rue Gynemer gate before Mike asked, "How much did you give those kids? It was fifty francs, wasn't it?"

"It was all I had."

They walked silently along the outside of the wrought iron fence. When they crossed the wide Rue de Vaugirard on a green light Mike said, "I'll flag down a cab."

"Don't bother," Judy answered him. "We're now on the Rue Bonaparte and it's only a few narrow blocks to where I live."

With comments now and again which failed to open up a conversation they strolled past the small stores, some still open but most now gated and shuttered for the night. Ahead of them Mike spotted Le Drugstore's neon sign, and felt Judy touch him on the arm. She pointed to the doorway of the small department store, and with something approaching distaste Mike saw that the pair of old tramps were now bedded down for the night, covered with a torn and dirty piece of canvas.

"Don't the police ever arrest them, or move them?" he asked her.

"On particularly cold nights a police car may stop and give them a ride to a warm cell for the night. They let them out again early in the morning. This is their turf. They bother nobody; nobody bothers them."

They turned the corner into the Boulevard St. Germain and halted at the door of Judy's hotel. Mike pressed some bills into her hand. "May I come up for a minute?" he asked.

"Not tonight, Mike."

"When can I see you again, Judy?"

"If I go home, I may see you in September," she answered, entering the foyer of the hotel and disappearing into its semi-darkness.

Mike flagged a cab, and angry and frustrated gave the driver the name of his hotel. They made a reckless left turn on a green light at the square, drove along Bonaparte to the quays and took the Pont du Caroussel to the Right Bank of the river.

The driver this time was a dour middle-aged man wearing a civilian blue peaked-cap, silent and yet somehow menacing as old bartenders and policemen often become. He had not spoken a word yet to his passenger, merely acknowledging Mike's earlier destination directions with a surly nod of his head.

Suddenly Mike leaned over the front seat and said, in English, "Take me back to where you picked me up."

There was another nod of the head, and they swung around the Louvre and the Tuileries, sped along the Rue de Rivoli, and fought their way through the heavy evening traffic in the Place de la Concorde. They re-crossed the river and drove along St. Germaine to the Brasserie Lipp.

Mike took a bill of large denomination from his wallet, wishing now that he'd kept some of the smaller bills he'd pressed into Judy's hand, and offered it across the back of the front seat.

"I 'ave no *change*, sir," the driver said, impassively staring straight ahead.

Mike looked around him for a waiter, considered changing the bill at the cashier's counter inside the restaurant, glanced at the driver's hard profile and the heavy gnarled hand clutching the money, and said, "Keep it."

Without a thank you the driver sped off.

Mike took an empty back corner table at the small sidewalk café, from which he had an unrestricted view of the front door of the Tar- anne, ordered himself a double Courvoisier, and sat there sipping it, somehow sensing that Judy would re-emerge from her hotel. He re-

51

membered her denying what he was thinking earlier in the evening, refusing to answer when he asked her if she had a lover, and her saying, ". . . no pretty girl ever starved to death in Paris." Whatever all this had meant, he was determined to find out.

Across the boulevard at the Café Flore a young girl with a small accordion or concertina was singing songs, and from the applause and laughter that wafted across to him he knew they were *risqué*. There was something familiar about the scene but it took him several minutes to remember the record album cover in his collection showing a very young Edith Piaf picking up a few francs singing in the streets like the young girl across the boulevard.

His cognac was almost finished when a Citroen limousine pulled into the curb in front of the Taranne's doorway and a black uniformed chauffeur sprang out, opened the back door and spoke to a large black man in a dinner jacket who was sitting in the back seat. With a salute the chauffeur shut the car's door again and made his way into the hotel. The man in the back seat disappeared into the anonymity of the car's interior.

In less than a minute the chauffeur re-appeared, holding the hotel door open to allow a gowned and stoled Judy Craig to make a stunningly beautiful exit from the hotel. The chauffeur ran across the sidewalk and opened the car's rear door for her, while at the same time Mike jumped up from his table, grabbed her arm and confronted her.

"What the hell do you mean spying on me!" she exclaimed contemptuously, breaking loose from him. The chauffeur ran back and stood at her side.

"It's all right, Olbo," she said to him in English. "This man used to be a friend of mine."

"Who's your new friend, a *black* African dictator?" Hammond asked sarcastically.

The chauffeur grabbed him by one of his biceps in a grip that almost made him cry out, and he was led to the open door of the car.

Judy said, "Your Majesty, I'd like you to meet a childhood friend of mine, Mr. Michael Hammond."

The big black figure in the back seat said, in a Sandhurst accent, "Nice to meet you, old boy. Any *past* friend of Judy's is also a friend of mine." Behind the luminous white-toothed smile was an implicit threat.

Judy took a wad of bills from her jewelled handbag and dropped them at Hammond's feet before being helped into the car. The chauffeur ran around and took his place at the wheel. The limousine made an imperious U-turn to glide away in the direction of the Quai d'Orsay or one of the fashionable streets in the 16th Arrondissement between l'Etoile and the Bois de Boulogne.

Hammond picked up the money he had given Judy earlier, and watched, open-mouthed, until the car disappeared in the traffic.

THE MAN WITH THE MUSICAL TOOTH

Of all the prisoners this jail has held, the only one I was ever sorry for was Thetford Culligan — and he was a murderer. There have only been five murderers in the Daleton lock-up since Confederation, two of them during the thirty years I've been town constable and turnkey. The first was Adam Bonnycastle who murdered his nephew for his money back in 1926. He was a bad one, and I was actually glad to see him go to the scaffold in the old bell tower. The other one was Thet Culligan who followed Bonnycastle the year before last.

Most people in the province have heard about the Culligan case, although the trial was as unsensational as Culligan's murder of his wife had been. There was no startling testimony, or vigorous pleas by the defense. Culligan admitted all along that he was guilty, and he even made the remark in court that the whole thing was a waste of time and money. It seemed to me, however, that the judge and crown counsel had failed to see the true motive for the crime. Not that it mattered much, because there was obvious incentive enough without it.

But let me begin at the beginning.

Late one night in the summer of 1949 my phone rang, and when I answered it a voice said, "This is the Provincial Police, Mr. Davis. There's been a murder over here in Tinsford, and the suspect will have to be lodged in your jail. We'll be bringing him over as soon as the inspector finishes his preliminary questioning."

Tinsford is a village about ten miles down the highway from Daleton, which is the county seat. I knew nearly everyone in the place, so I asked, "Who was killed?"

"A young woman by the name of Culligan. Crinny Culligan," the policeman answered.

"And who's the suspect?"

"The woman's husband."

"Not Thet Culligan!"

"That's right. Do you know him?"

"Why, yes," I answered. "Everybody around here knows him. He's the one they call The Man With The Musical Tooth. Maybe I'd better come down there."

I hung up, pulled on my clothes, and drove down the highway through the teeming rain to the Culligan place, just the other side of the village. When I arrived there I found two Provincial Police cars in the yard. I made myself known to the Police Inspector, and he led me into the untidy little parlor of the house. Thet Culligan was sitting on a shabby studio couch against the wall, his head buried in his hands.

I'd seen the man perhaps twenty times before, and every time he'd looked exactly the same. He was a short insignificant-looking little fellow who seemed to go through life like an apologetic mouse through a cheese factory. He was a man about fifty years of age, who almost always wore an oversized blue serge suit. Tonight his suit was topped by a not-too-clean white collar and a flamboyant red and yellow tie. Above the necktie his adam's apple supported his long head like a ball and socket, and his sparse hair was combed across his bald pate in a clumsy attempt at camouflage.

"Hello, Thetford," I greeted him.

He looked up quickly. "Hello, Mr. Davis." He appeared happy to have found someone he knew among all the strange policemen.

"What happened?" I asked.

"I killed Crinny," he answered, lowering his head once again into his hands.

One of the Provincials took me upstairs. There were a couple of plainclothesmen taking photographs and measurements in the back bedroom of the small house. The room showed signs of a struggle, and Thet's young wife, Crinny, was lying across the bed, one slippered foot touching the floor. Her other slipper was clutched in her right hand, as if she'd been using it for a weapon to defend herself. She'd been strangled to death, apparently, as indicated by the bruises on her throat.

The Police Inspector questioned Culligan again for an hour or so, but all he could get out of him was, "I killed her. There's no use asking me all this stuff. I choked her to death right up there on the bed."

They brought him up to Daleton in one of the police cars, and I put him in a cell in the empty jail house. Then I phoned home and told the wife I'd have to stay there with him the rest of the night, but to get on the phone to young Bert McCready, who helped me out as an assistant when we had a prisoner, and tell him to get down to the jail by eight in the morning.

The Provincials took everything out of Thet's pockets, and also removed his necktie, shoelaces and belt. He handed the stuff over without a murmur, but he smiled a little when they took away his belt.

"Are they afraid I might hang myself, Mr. Davis?" he asked.

"There's no telling, Thet," I said. "It's just a regualtion."

"Am I allowed to smoke?"

"Sure. I'll bring you your cigarettes as soon as I put your other things away in the office, and enter them up in the personal effects book."

I locked him up, and showed the Provincials to the front door. When I got back to the cell corridor he was pacing up and down his cell, staring at the floor. His thin face was deeply lined and sad-looking, and his hands were trembling, one of them clenched at his side.

I handed him a lighted cigarette through the bars, and he asked eagerly, "Do you remember the time I found out about my gift, Mr. Davis?"

I sat down in a chair across the corridor from his cell and answered, "Sure, Thet, I remember quite well."

He smiled like an old prize fighter who wants to remember nothing but his triumphs. "What happened tonight started way back then," he said, lowering himself to the cot fastened against the wall. His voice belied his looks. It was strong and sure, and mirrored an intelligence not apparent in his outward appearance.

"You don't need to say anything to me unless you want to," I warned him.

"I'd like to tell you the whole story, Mr. Davis, if you'll listen. I won't be able to sleep anyhow, and it may help me if I get it off my chest."

"I'd like to hear it, Thet," I said. "I've only heard bits of it before this."

He was silent for a minute or two, taking long puffs of his cigarette. Then he began to talk.

"It was the ninth of July, nineteen-forty-one. I came here to Daleton to have a couple of teeth filled. I'll never forget it. It was a hot afternoon, and because I was a little scared of old Doc Bailey's drill I dropped in to the Daleton House for a beer or two first. I met a fellow name of Charley Stone who used to buy cattle around here, and we sat for an hour or two drinking beer and eating the peanuts they used to put on the tables in them days."

He looked at me and I nodded.

"When I left Charley I walked up to Doc Bailey's as brave as a lion, and he sat me down in his chair. Well, sir, I kidded with the Doc — he was a fine old man was Doc Bailey — and when he drilled them teeth I didn't feel a thing. After he finished filling them, I paid him and walked out of his office, hoping to run into Charley again before I went home.

"I was walking down Main Street, right over there in front of the five-and-ten, when I began to hear music. It wasn't very loud, but I could hear every note, just as if it was coming from a loudspeaker. Well, sir, I thought it must be coming from the radio store, and I didn't pay much attention. I stayed here in town until it got dark, before going back to my place. I was batching it then — remember? — up the road from where we — from my new house.

"All the way home I could hear the music playing, and sometimes there would be a speaker or an announcement. I remember there was a man talking about the German army advancing into Russia —"

He looked through the bars to see if I was listening, and I motioned to him to keep going.

"All that night I could hear the music. It seemed to follow me everywhere I went. At first I thought it was the effects of the beer, but after I'd eaten my supper I knew it wasn't that. I began to get scared. I walked outside, but I couldn't get away from it. I had an old horse then, and I went out to the stable and talked to him." He looked up again. "You must think I was batty, and I thought so too, at the time. It was an awful thing, trying to get away from that music and them speeches. Well, around midnight the music faded, and though I could hear it bump-bump-bumping, it was much farther away.

"I stayed awake half the night listening to it. There was one orchestra after another from all over the United States. I don't know what time I fell asleep, but it must have been pretty near dawn. I woke up to find the sun away up in the sky, and I could hear my old horse stamping in his stall.

"For a few minutes I didn't notice anything, but soon I heard a man and woman arguing right near to me. After listening to them for a minute or two I realized it was a radio serial I heard. I couldn't eat my breakfast for thinking about it. I could hear it plain as day, and when it finished and the announcer began talking about some soap powder, I began to laugh." He stopped talking and looked out at me in the apologetic way he had. I gave him another cigarette before he went on.

"All that day I listened to the programs. During the afternoon my sister Daisy came over to get me to drive her here to town, and I asked her if she could hear a radio playing. She listened, and said she could. I sure was relieved then. At least I knew it wasn't only me. It wasn't only something wrong with my head. You understand how I felt?"

I told him I understood.

"When I drove Daisy here to Daleton we asked her kids if they could hear any music. They began to dance around and look all over the buggy for the radio. I was happy then for the first time since it had started.

"We drove into town, and Daisy went into the bank. I stayed outside and listened to the radio. People passed me on the sidewalk, and I nodded to one or two of them. They didn't hear anything, I knew, because they never let on, and they would have asked me what I was doing with a radio in the buggy if they had, especially Mrs. Flossie Murdoch.

"Well, sir, I listened to my radio for two or three days. I wasn't scared any more, just kind of — bewildered. In the daytime I could get two or three Toronto stations and sometimes Hamilton or Buffalo, but late at night I listened to KDKA Pittsburgh, WLW Cincinnati, and later on, when I learned how to operate it, I once got Los Angeles, California, about two o'clock in the morning —"

"Operate it?" I interrupted, wondering whether there might not be something wrong with his head after all.

"Sure," he answered, smiling at me. "But I'll tell you about that when I come to it.

"Let's see, I guess it was about the third day that I found out the music was coming from my tooth. You may think I was slow in finding it out, and it's hard to explain to people how it was. Suppose you heard music all around you all the time — radio music — and quiz programs and dramas and advertisements — " He paused and fixed his eyes on me. "Would you think it was coming from one of your teeth?"

I shook my head. "How did you find out?" I asked him.

59

"From eating. When I was eating, the music stopped, or went only in fits and starts. I found that when I had a mouthful of food I couldn't hear the radio. I know it sounds simple, but it took me three days to discover it. Then I tested the new fillings in my teeth with my tongue until I knew which one it was. With my tongue I couldn't stop it altogether, but I could blot out certain stations. That's how I learned to tune it."

I found myself running my tongue over one or two ancient fillings in my own back teeth, and wondering how he had felt when he discovered he was a human receiving set. I suppose the realization would have floored almost anybody. "Did it keep you awake every night?" I asked him.

"At first it did, but I learned to go to sleep and forget about it.

"What bothered me most was that nobody would believe me when I told them about it. I went down to Tapper's store in Tinsford one morning and just stood at the counter and opened my mouth. Old Sam Tapper came along the counter to take my order. I told him to send some groceries out to my place, and he began writing my order in his book. Suddenly he stopped writing, looked up at the ceiling, and said, 'The old lady's sure got that danged radio on loud this morning.' I started laughing, and Sam just stood there, wondering what for. 'It's me, Sam,' I said to him. 'I'm a human radio.'

"Well, sir, it took me the best part of half an hour to convince Sam. Finally I had to give a demonstration to his missus. George Slater, and one or two others I've forgot, came in too. Before long they half believed me, but I could see they still thought it was a trick.

"During the next week or so I showed pretty near everybody here in town. I used to drive in every day from my place. Mrs. Flossie Murdoch even made me show the Baptist minister, before she'd believe her ears. One day a young lad came to see me from the *Times-Spectator* and wrote a story about me for the paper. It was a good story, even if it was colored a bit, and there was pictures of me and Doc Bailey. People began to stop me on the street – some that wouldn't have noticed me the week before. I showed everybody my tooth, and let them listen in. Even Mr. Darling from the bank spoke to me, and listened for a while."

He paused in his story, and sat silent for a full minute on the edge of the cot. Then he got to his feet and began to pace the length of the cell, one hand grasping his trousers to keep them from sliding to the floor. I leaned back in my chair against the wall of the corridor and watched him. I could see now that his story, despite its humor, was a tragic one. It was the tragedy of the clown — of the little man catapulted from obscurity by something beyond his control; something that had to be ridiculous enough to make the world take heed.

He sat down again. "I guess you remember the stories they printed about me in the papers?" he asked.

I nodded.

"One city paper sent a woman out here. She was very nice, but she made me speak real slow so she could put everything down on a pad. Crinny was like that. Women don't seem to be able to remember . . ." His voice trailed off. "Did you see her?" he asked.

I nodded again.

"I really didn't mean to hurt her — at first," he said. "I'd never hurt her before. Not once." Then after a pause he asked, "Was she — did she — was she still pretty?"

I said that she was. I was afraid he was going to cry. "Please go on," I begged him.

He was alone with his thoughts, and didn't hear me. I looked out of the small barred window behind me and noticed that the rain had stopped.

He began again. "After the stories in the papers it seemed that nearly everybody began to write me. Some people wrote me letters saying I was crazy. A woman away down in Norfolk, Virginia, said she had had a dream about me, and wanted me to go there and let her be my first disciple. There was a lot of letters asking me to put on shows for clubs. One fellow asked me to go into partners with him in a medicine show. Some of the letters were real nice. A lot of people had read the stories in the papers, and thought I wanted to stop my tooth from being a radio." He looked over at me. "I never could figure out why they thought I wanted it to stop. I guess it was because the stories told about me not being able to sleep nights at first."

I asked him to tell me more about the letters he'd received. He thought for a minute or two and then, his face lighting up with his sad

61

quiet smile, he said, "One man advised me to gargle four times a day with oil of cloves and water. And a radio mechanic in Detroit told me to ground my tooth on a bare 110 volt wire. A lady in Quebec City said that what I heard was astral voices, and to try to contact her dead husband who'd been a dentist.

"I guess I must have got fifty letters telling me different ways to stop it, but not one of them advised me to have the tooth pulled."

He laughed his quiet laugh, and I joined with him, forgetting for a moment who we were, and what he had done.

"There was reporters from a lot of big city papers came up that summer to see me," he went on. "They used to stay here at the Daleton House. One time there was two here together from the States, one of them, Mr. Rollins, from a New York paper, and another one called Sleight who was writing a piece about me for a magazine. We sure had a lot of fun together. Sleight was the only man I ever seen put salt *and* pepper in his beer.

"One time I got a phone call in the middle of the night from England – I was staying over at the Daleton House then; Mr. Greerson gave me room and board free after the reporters started to come – well, this phone call was from the *London Daily Mail*. I let them hear my radio over the phone."

There was something quite simple and pathetic in his pride about these things. I knew that whatever happened later, I could never joke about the things he was telling me. It would be like making fun of a person having to push himself around in a wheelchair.

He told me of being featured in a Believe It Or Not cartoon, and of the offer he'd received to appear at a Texas exposition. There had been examinations by representatives of both the dental and radio professions, and he described them to me at some length, especially one conducted by a professor from Toronto University and another by an engineer from the Massachusetts Institute of Technology. He had never found out what their findings had been. All he knew was that they'd wrapped him up in wires "like a Christmas tree" in order to prove that his dental amalgam was a miniature radio receiving set, a fact of which he was very much aware.

He had made a few local stage appearances, finally being summoned to New York where he performed on a radio show. Following this he'd toured the U.S. Middle West as a Chautauqua and third-rate vaudeville performer.

When I asked him what kind of act he'd given on the stage, he answered, "What they used to do was stand me in front of a microphone, and I'd tell them about my gift — that's what they called it — give them a demonstration of how it worked, and go down into the audience to let people authentificate that it was really coming from my tooth."

I stopped him. "I don't want to interrupt, Thet, but how did you learn to turn it on and off?"

"Oh, didn't I tell you yet? I did it with chewing gum. When I didn't want it to play I just stuck a wad of gum over the filling. It worked good too. I guess I found out about the gum a week or so after it started.

"I stayed in vaudeville for nearly a year. I didn't make an awful lot of money, but I came back to Tinsford with about twenty-five hundred dollars.

"I guess I was the most famous person around here then," he went on wistfully. "Everybody invited me to their parties. That's where I met Crinny, at a party. She was only twenty then, and I was, let's see, forty-one. I guess her head was turned by all the attention I got. She was sure a pretty kid. She was the prettiest girl around this part of the country.

He stood up again, but he must have realized that it was ridiculous trying to walk around while clutching his trousers. With a small apologetic smile he sat down again on the cot. Outside, the sky was beginning to brighten, and I could see two or three stars uncovered by the scudding clouds.

"I bought the place we're — the place we lived in, that year, and we got married. We were happy at first — at least I was — but it didn't take me long to see I'd made a mistake marrying a girl as young as that. I worked the few acres that went with the house, and did some carpentering, making enough money to live on, but we never seemed to have enough. Crinny was a Hyslop, you know. The whole family of them began sponging off me as soon as we were married. I didn't mind that so much, but what bothered me most was the way Crinny used to get me to perform for all kinds of people. Whenever any of her young friends would come to see her, she'd ask me to put on a show

63

for them, and after I was finished, they'd all laugh. They'd laugh *at* me. Do you understand what I mean, Mr. Davis? If it hadn't been for my tooth none of them would have even spoke to me."

He broke off, and his hands searched habitually through his empty pockets. I handed him a cigarette, and lighted it through the bars. After taking a couple of puffs he began again.

"When this thing first started, people treated it serious, but now I was back home everybody thought it was a great joke like – like if my wife was going with another man. You know, one of them secret jokes that everybody knows but you. Mr. Darling from the bank didn't speak to me no more, and neither did the others who'd only spoke to me when I was – " He searched his mind for the right word.

"An attraction," I ventured.

"Yes, that's what I mean. Well, sir, after that things were pretty quiet. You know, Crinny and me never had any children. Maybe things might have been different if we had, but Crinny wouldn't have any. All she wanted was a good time. Evenings in the summer she'd go down to the city or somewheres with two or three other young people. There was one fellow, Graham Walker, that took her out quite a bit too. It used to bother me some, but I couldn't go dancing and things every night like they did."

He leaned back and took a long drag of his cigarette. "Have you ever wondered why I never got my tooth fixed?" he asked.

The question was rather unexpected. "Why didn't you, Thet?"

"It's hard to say. I guess my tooth was all I had. It was the same as being red-headed or able to play the piano. I was different – you know what I mean?"

I nodded.

"Not only that, neither. I got interested in a lot of things. No matter what I was doing, or where I was, I could still listen to the radio. I learned a different thing every day. I got to like good music, and I listened to all the speakers. Some nights, when Crinny was away, I used to lay there in bed and listen to all the news broadcasts. I liked Edward R. Murrow, Gabriel Heatter and H.V. Kaltenborn. Well, sir, soon it seemed I knew more about what was going on in the world than anybody else around this district."

I began to see how this thing had changed his whole life. I understood now why he'd been surprised and shocked at the suggestions made by well-meaning people who advised him how to stop it.

When he began again his voice was pitched lower than before, and his clenched fist beat softly against the leg of his blue serge trousers. "Once I got one of them unsigned letters telling me that Crinny was having Graham Walker out to the house all the time when I was away. Them kind of things can bother you terrible, but I never let on to Crinny that I knew ..."

The sky was now morning bright outside, and I could hear the sound of early morning traffic from the street.

"One time I asked Crinny if it wasn't time she stopped seeing Graham Walker; that people were beginning to talk. She told me all the talk going around about them was a pack of lies, and I should be ashamed to think any different. Then she began to cry.

"There isn't much more to tell. Last night there was five or six young people out at my place, including Walker. I went up to my room early, sick of their silly talk and crazy dancing. Crinny came up after a while and asked me to show one of them, that hadn't seen it before, how my tooth worked. I didn't feel like going, but I didn't want to disappoint her neither. I went down and put on my act, but my tooth didn't work so good. I guess it was the storm. Anyways, all I could get was a lot of static.

"After the others had gone, Crinny came upstairs and shoved her head into my room. She said I'd made a fool of her in front of her friends. I explained that it wasn't my fault the tooth didn't work so good. She argued that I'd done it on purpose. It wasn't much of an argument at first, but you know how these married squabbles start with nothing and then get serious. She said a lot of mean things to me then, bragging about what had gone on between her and Graham Walker, and threatening to run away with him in the morning ...

"I don't remember very clear what both of us said after that, but everything I've told you tonight kept coming back to me. Crinny was screaming, and she took off one of her slippers and hit me as hard as she could in the jaw with it. I knocked her down on my bed then, and my hands went to her neck. I guess I went crazy, and I just kept pressing and pressing until she stopped struggling and lay still ... "

65

I leaned over and picked some cigarette butts from the floor.

"Do you think they'll keep me here until the fall assizes?" Thetford asked.

"It's likely, Thet," I answered.

"I hope they get it over with quick," he said, his eyes roving around the small cell. There's nothing else to live for now." He sighed. "It's sure funny how things turn out. If it hadn't been for my tooth, none of this would have ever happened."

I was more sorry for him than I've ever been for another man before or since. To try to cheer him up a bit I said, "Well, anyway, Thet, you'll be glad you have your radio now. It'll make the time before your trial pass a little quicker."

He stared at me in surprise. Then he shook his head sadly and unclenched his fist. In the palm of his hand lay a minute piece of metal that had been the filling in his tooth.

"Crinny knocked it out with the slipper," he said sadly. "That was the only reason I killed her, I guess."

LOSERS WEEPERS

It rained the day they buried Archie Randolph, a cold sleety rain that turned the cemetery lawns into soft sago pudding. The few footprints in the grass leading from the paved road to the graveside were muddy indentations which the sleet was unable to hide. That Archie would be buried on such a day was an odds-on bet to any of us who knew him or might have remembered him.

Strangely to some, I still called Archie an acquaintance, which seemed to those who had once known him a silly thing to admit. Almost the only thing most of those who'd known Archie will own up to is that he was a genuine one-hundred-percent creep. My medical dictionary defines a psycopath as "One with a constitutional lack of moral sensibility, although possessing a normal intelligence," which describes Archie Randolph to a T. His widest group of acquaintances was made up of male suckers from whom he'd stolen, begged or "borrowed" money — and women. He really hated women, with a close-to-the-surface hatred that the rest of us just didn't understand.

Back in the fifties, before I was barred from the Press Club for life, I split my considerable leisure time between the Club and a lower Bay Street pub called the Safari. After I was turfed out of the Club I no longer had to share my patronage between the two drinking spots but could concentrate on the Safari alone. For some reason or another Archie Randolph moved himself over to the beer parlor too. Archie had a revealing habit perhaps known only to me, for I never passed the information on to anyone else. When he was about to tell one of his frequent lies he would swallow unnecessarily first. I spotted this early in our acquaintance at the Press Club when I stood beside him at the bar and listened to him take a new member for one of his frequent phony "loans."

Archie said to the young fellow, dry swallowing first, "It's only because the banks are closed, of course. I only need the ten dollars to see me through the evening. You'll get it back tomorrow noon."

"No hurry," the sucker replied, taking a bill from his wallet that Archie received with his usual careless aplomb. "I may not be in the Club for the next few days."

"Okay. The next time I see you then," Archie said.

"No hurry," the young man repeated.

To me it sounded like the last useless protestation of a person being led the the gallows — or the cleaners.

We used to have a table near the service bar at the rear of the men's beverage room in the Safari, up against the dropped partition that separated the Men Only beer parlor from the Ladies & Escorts Room, as they used to call it then. This open-topped partition inhibited most of the customers at our table, but I was constantly getting myself cut off or kicked out for too-loud swearing. Let's face it, I was always a wet service canteen drinker. One time the whole table, around which we'd often have as many as seven or eight chairs instead of the usual four, was cut off because we were singing obscene wartime limericks to the tune of *Sing Us Another One Do.*

Over the next few years, until they tore out both the men's and ladies' rooms and turned the whole ground floor into a posh cocktail lounge for the briefcase and sideburn set, our table drew a steady but constantly fluid clientele of *Toronto Telegram* newspapermen, salesmen, bums, unemployed lushes, and guys who had mysterious jobs in public relations or as advertising account executives. Archie Randolph who had earned few honest dollars since leaving prep school, was *always* at the table. I mentioned the old Safari men's beer parlor because it was there where most of his past acquaintances or friends met Archie, got taken for drinks or loans, and learned to hate him. I remember in particular the afternoon when he made the remark that stunned us all, and was an exceptionally rotten one even for him. He said, "Well, they took mother to the hospital this morning, so it may not be too long before I get my hands on the estate." From then on it would have been useless for him to deny the fact, he was just waiting for his mother to die.

His mother, whom none of us had ever met, had always been good to him — too good most of us thought. She had always kept him well dressed and in drinking money, giving him what really amounted to a regular remittance. As far as his drinking was concerned I've got to admit that he carried his drinks much better than I ever could. He always remained slim and dressed in an ultra-conservative style: dark business suits, white shirts, subdued neckties, black socks, highly polished black shoes, the whole Establishment shmeer. His hair in those days was clipped fairly short with a side part, black curly hair that attracted a great many women. His looks were distinguished by a weak chin and petulant mouth, though he could be utterly charming, especially towards women, when charm was a necessary part of his schemes against them. One incident will serve to illustrate what I mean.

I forget now what year it was but one afternoon he asked me to accompany him to a downtown supper club where he was to meet a fellow Safari drinker and his wife for dinner. Knowing Archie as I did I made sure he was paying for the meal before agreeing to go with him.

The dinner was a huge success — for Archie. He turned on the charm to the beautiful young wife of our mutual drinking companion, an advertising copywriter who lived in a west-of-the-city suburb, and even I could sense her melting acknowledgment of it. Her husband, whom Archie plied with drinks, became almost a boor when stacked against the two.

Archie would say something like, "I suppose you've seen the Gregory show at the Pitcairn Gallery, Charity?" Charity, the beautiful but unsophisticated little wife, would shake her head, probably not even knowing where the Pitcairn was or even of its existence up to then. "You should get Ralph to take you; it's well worth a trip in from Islington," Archie would say, bringing to her attention the fact that Ralph Collat had not only banished her to a bungalow in suburbia but was unable to notice her potential as an essentially cultured young woman.

It was clever, and I was fascinated by Archie's approach as I'm continually fascinated by the clinch line in any con-man's story. Archie was a con artist all his life, utterly ruthless and forgetful of his victims once they were taken by him, his mind working ahead to the next mark on his list. While he worked his hustle however he concentrated on it exclusively, not for one second letting go of the charming self-portrait he was implanting in the sucker's mind.

After we'd finished dinner I tried to bring the evening to an end by getting up to leave. Archie pulled me down into my chair and said, "Bill, what's wrong? You've already phoned Donna. It's scarcely seven-thirty." Archie knew all of our wives by their first names.

Ralph Collat joined in drunkenly. "Sure. What do you want to be a party-pooper for, Bill? Archie's right."

I glanced across the table at the poor slob and wondered why I'd allowed myself to be conned into becoming Archie Randolph's shill.

It was only a momentary twitch of conscience however, for no married man with a pretty wife and a modicum of common sinse would have allowed her within a half mile of Archie.

In my own case I'd taken Archie home with me only once, before I really knew him. When I found out what he was like I warned Randolph that if he ever phoned my wife or dropped by as if by chance to see me I'd not only fill him in, but also put in a quick phone call to his mother. Archie understood a direct threat when he heard one, and I think he rather admired my lack of subtlety. Anyhow my wife Donna had seen right through his phony charm on his one visit to our house.

By the time the dinner party broke up Archie had charmed Charity Collat completely, while making her husband appear to be a drunken lout who was unworthy of being married to her. Outside the club I flagged a cab, and as I got in I saw Archie persuading Ralph to lie down on the back seat of Randolph's black Pontiac, and then graciously opening the front door so that Charity could sit next to him as he drove the couple home. At the time I wasn't quite sure just what the con was, but knew that part of it would be the seduction of the exceptionally beautiful Charity Collat. Archie may have also had the idea of taking the young couple for one of his infamous "loans," but subsequent events rubbed it out. To cut a long story to size, about two weeks after the dinner with the Collats Archie took Charity on a mid-winter flight to Bermuda, leaving behind a thoroughly distraut and bewildered young husband who became drunk daily somewhere even before the Safari opened its doors at noon.

From then on Collat sat alone at a table at the other end of the room from his friends, brooding over his beers. The rest of us resolved to cut Randolph dead if he showed his face in the beer parlor again. This was agreed with heartily by Johnny Dixon the floor manager, who had been defrauded out of a "loan" by Archie months before. Dixon went even further, and after talking things over with Mr. Bluemann the Safari's owner, assured us all that Archie would never again be allowed to step inside the place.

Whatever happened in Bermuda, Charity Collat flew home after a week, leaving Archie behind. I only saw her once after her return, and then only to offer my condolences, but I noticed that she'd suddenly changed into a life-hardened mature woman in contrast to the naive young bride I'd met over dinner three weeks before.

The day after his wife's return Ralph Collat took his own life by throwing himself in front of a subway train, and it was at *his* funeral, which I'm proud to say about twenty of his Safari friends attended, that I spoke briefly to his widow. I heard later that Charity (they had no children, thank God) had sold the bungalow in Islington and had returned to the small Western town where her parents lived.

From then on Archie Randolph — who in his congenital inability to ever see himself as others saw him had made one abortive attempt to re-enter the Safari — now drank at a smaller downtown pub, which until the Safari changed itself into a cocktail lounge the rest of us had studiously avoided.

A few years later, when the only times I ran into Archie were widely spaced occasions indeed, I talked with a radio station manager who had attended the same fashionable prep school as Randolph, and had known him well.

"Was Randolph ever married?" I asked this former friend.

"Yes, and guess who he suckered into becoming his best man, and also paying the caterer?" he answered, pointing to himself. "He was married for a very brief time to Therese Michelin, who was then a well-known portrait painter. Whether they were subsequently divorced or not I don't know, but she had plenty of grounds, believe me. What he did to poor Therese's psyche I don't know either, but I know he ruined her as a painter. Did you ever see any of her earlier work?"

I shook my head. "I'm not really up on the painting scene," I told him.

"She was great, really great, Bill. One-woman New York exhibitions, that sort of thing. After Archie there was nothing. I haven't even heard her name in years."

After the Safari changed its downstairs image a few of our back table habitués took their patronage to the pub where Archie drank, among them a wild-laughing, wild-looking young guy we called Kooky, who'd spent three years in a German P.O.W. camp following the raid on Dieppe. Though he knew better, he was probably too drunk at the time to care, and Kooky let Randolph take him for fifty dollars out of one of his monthly pension cheques. Kooky, who worked rather infrequently and received the pension for a heart condition attributed to the prison camp, almost starved before his next cheque came through. All Archie gave him to survive on were a daily series of promises, none of which he ever kept.

I'd heard at second hand about Randolph taking Kooky, but one day after we'd put my magazine to bed I dropped into the Safari bar for a drink. I mentioned the story about Kooky and Randolph to Jake, one of the bartenders. In a few minutes an Italian cocktail waiter named Leonardo, who had been a beer waiter before the switch, came over and talked to me as I sat on a bar stool. He asked me about Kooky, and I told him what I'd heard.

"That son of a bitch!" Then he said, "Thanks, Bill. How's the family?"

"Great, Lenny. How's yours?"

He held up three fingers, and I laughed. In the Safari's beer parlor days he'd fathered only one baby.

Later that week three men in working clothes jumped Archie Randolph in a parking lot behind his pub and worked him over good, putting him in St. Michael's Hospital with three broken ribs, facial cuts and contusions and a groin injury. Archie told the police he'd never seen any of the men before, but that they were Italian. That didn't help much for we have more than a quarter of a million Italians in the city. Now I remembered that Randolph had once taken Leonardo for twenty dollars, and that the Italian waiter and Kooky had been pretty good friends.

The second last time I ever talked with Archie Randolph was about a year after he'd been beaten up in the parking lot. It was a Saturday afternoon, and I'd taken my wife and daughter to lunch in Chinatown. Following lunch the women had gone clothes-ogling through the department stores, and that's where I'd checked out. I told my wife I'd see her later at home, and on an impulse I decided to have a beer in the pub which some of the old gang, including Randolph, now frequented.

The place was more than half empty, most of the tables occupied by solitary elderly drinkers, the weekend papers clutched under their arms. At a table at the rear of the joint I spied Alan Grouper, one of the old Safari crowd, who'd made a career of sorts by selling everything from advertising blurbs for telephone pads to memberships in a group that promised cut-rate airline fares for salesmen. Alan had flown Halifax bombers for the R.C.A.F. twenty years before, but had been flying much higher ever since on his get-rich schemes. I was just about to walk up the room and join Alan and some guy with a beard he was talking to when a voice at my elbow said, "Hi, Bill."

I turned and found Archie Randolph sitting alone at a front corner table. He was still as immaculate as ever, but now his face had attained the pink patina of the chronic drunk. I sat down facing him across the table.

"How's things, Bill?" he asked me. "You're not in the magazine editing caper any more?"

"No. I gave it up when the book went from a weekly to a monthly."

"You look fairly prosperous."

"I get by."

"How's Donna?"

I didn't even bother answering him.

As if he hadn't noticed he asked, "And the kids?"

"Both married, both with kids of their own."

"Jesus, we're getting old," he said, draining his glass.

When the waiter came Archie insisted the beer was on him, and to my surprise he even tipped the waiter.

"How come, Archie?" I asked. "You given up your old lifestyle?"

He grinned his old fraudulent grin and answered, "I'm putting myself back in the management's good books. I was cut off from here for a month, and just got myself reinstated last week."

"What for, the usual?"

It was his turn to ignore a question.

He took a slow sip of his beer and said, "You'll probably hear the wrong version of it somewhere so I'll tell you what happened." Whatever it was he was obviously eager to tell it. Knowing Archie as I did I knew that it would not be to excuse it but to live the incident over in its telling, to savor it again. I sipped my own beer and waited.

"I was drinking here with an idiot I'd never even met before. It was after five o'clock on a Friday and the place was crowded. The only empty seat was at this fellow's table, so I took it. He told me he only dropped in for a beer after work on Fridays; he was a maintenance man or something of the sort over on York Street." He sipped his drink.

73

"There were a couple of other people at the table, stock exchange people maybe." He swallowed, and I knew a lie was coming. "Well, this janitor bought me a beer and began talking about the National League pennant race or something. I wasn't the least bit interested. I was waiting for a chair to be vacated at one of the tables up front where Kooky and a couple of the old Bay Street crowd were sitting – "

"Don't tell me Kooky still drinks with you, after the dirty shabby fuckin trick you pulled on him!"

"Of course! Why not?" he asked me angrily. He gave me a mocking grin. "I guess you're referring to the loan he once gave me?"

"Gave you is right, you unprincipled middle class bastard!"

His eyes narrowed, but he said, "Kooky got that money back a long time ago, before I came out – when I was in the hospital a couple of months after borrowing it from him. I was short at the time or I'd have paid him right away, but my mother and my sister Eva were in Europe."

"The only reason you paid him back, and I suppose Leonardo too, was that you knew if you didn't those Eyeties were going to wait for you again and break your legs."

While he took an angry gulp of his beer I asked, "What about this guy the janitor?"

His anger had put more petulance around his mouth but he went on with his story. "I've already told you this guy was an idiot, and that his baseball talk bored hell out of me. Believe me, I wouldn't have talked to him at all if the only empty chair in the place hadn't been at his table.

"Go on."

"This fellow, the janitor or whatever the hell he was, took a small bill from a pay envelope he was carrying. You know, one of those small brown envelopes with a bank's advertising that some companies use when they pay wages or salaries in cash."

I nodded.

"He shoved this envelope into a side pocket of his jacket." Archie paused and took a drink of beer, giving himself a legitimate excuse to swallow this time. "I guess he must have pulled the pay envelope out of his pocket when he took out his cigarettes. Anyhow, after he left I found the pay envelope on the floor."

"Under your shoe, Randolph?"

He glared at me but went on. "A little later I joined some of the boys near the back of the room. The next time I went to the washroom I took the money out of the pay envelope — " He paused, wearing his psychopath's smile and waiting for me to comment. When I didn't he said, "I flushed the envelope down a toilet and put the money in my wallet."

"Did the man come back looking for it?"

"Apparently he did, later on. I'd left to keep a dinner engagement. I didn't even know the guy, Bill. You don't think I'd have turned in something I'd found on the floor to the manager of this joint, do you?"

"No, that'd have been the honest way to play it," I answered with contempt. "So you went to dinner on some poor working stiff's money. For chrissakes, man, haven't you any idea at all what it means to a working man to lose his whole week's pay!"

"It wasn't that much. Anyhow it was his own fault for being so careless."

I shook my head, holding myself from decking him right there.

"Oh come on, Bill," he said. "You've heard the saying, 'Finders keepers, losers weepers,' haven't you? I suppose *you've* never kept something you found?"

"Listen, you jeezly creep, don't try to ring *me* in as the same kind of bastard you are! How come they found out you had the poor guy's money anyway?"

"One of the stock exchange jerks at the table told Oscar the waiter he'd seen me pick up the envelope." He gave a dry swallow. "He hadn't of course. They even tried to claim I *stole* the guy's money at first. Nobody could prove anything against me, so now I've been reinstated here."

I stood up.

"You've still got half a glass of beer," Randolph wailed.

"Drink it yourself, or better still, stuff it."

"Where are you going, Bill?"

"Anywhere that you're not," I said.

The next and last time I saw Archie Randolph was a couple of years ago. My wife and I were having an after-show supper with another couple in a downtown steakhouse when a slightly tipsy but immaculate

Archie Randolph invited himself to our table and ordered a round of drinks. After acknowledging his greeting Donna excused herself and took the other woman to the powder room.

"Someone told me you were in the real estate business, Archie," I said.

He nodded, giving my friend and me his superior insolent grin. "It beats printing your own money," he said.

My friend, Jim Davidson, who's in the office supply business, spoke up eagerly. "My wife Lorrie and I are in the market for a house," he said. "Where is this development of yours, Mr. Randolph?"

I tried to give Jim a cautionary kick on the ankle but missed.

Archie told him where his company's development was being built, and handed Jim one of his embossed cards. "Give me a call, Mr. Davidson," he said. "Or better still, you and Lorrie drop out to see me. Believe me, this is the prestige buy of a lifetime. I can offer you a real deal on a split level we call our 'Ambassador'. Three bedrooms, double brick garage, sun-decked roof and flagstone patio, electric heat, on a corner lot with a ravine at the back. We're only fifteen minutes from the Metro limits."

"And only another thirty from the Metro limits to you office, Jim," I chimed in.

Archie laughed. "What I've always admired about Bill was his unflagging skepticism," he said.

We chatted about some of the old members of the Safari gang who'd died over the past few years, from heart attacks, drowning, cancer, meningitis, and one of the younger ones from peritonitis.

"And don't forget Ralph Collat's suicide," I put in.

Archie ignored that. Making one of the few percipient comments I'd ever heard from him Randolph said, "The funny part of it is that none of them died from cirrhosis of the liver. This either proves the medical fraternity wrong, or proves we were a lucky or durable bunch."

Archie told Jim and me that he was now living with a young black girl called Semantha Strong, who was filling out a long, constantly renewed engagement at a supper club out near the airport.

"Really!" Jim exclaimed, who'd been conditioned by twenty years of suburban marriage to be enviably amazed at such things.

"Don't ruin her, Randolph, as you ruined all the others," I said.

Archie gave me his mock-innocent, open-mouthed stare, then asked, "Such as who?"

"Let's take Therese Michelin and Charity Collat for starters."

He laughed. It was strained but it still came off as a laugh. "They were both dumb. Don't forget I didn't leave *them*, they left me."

"I wonder what for?"

Archie told Jim, "Semantha has them all fooled. She's a lousy singer really, and just lucky she's black. If she was a white girl she wouldn't even make a church choir."

Our wives returned before I had a chance to say what I really wanted to to the creep. I could imagine the opportunities he now had to humiliate sadistically someone of the opposite sex, especially since the Strong girl was vulnerable as a member of a minority group. I expected soon to hear of Randolph's death at the hands of a Black man.

After a couple of minutes of plying Lorrie Davidson with attention and phony charm Archie rose from the table. "I'm sorry, folks, but I have to pick up Semantha at the club after her last show." He gave Lorrie and Donna two charming farewells, shook hands with Davidson, reminding him to give him a call soon, said, "I'll be seeing you, Bill," and left the steakhouse.

As soon as he was gone Lorrie Davidson turned to Donna. "I don't see how you can think all the horrible things you do about Mr. Randolph. To me he's one of the most charming gentlemen I've ever met."

Her husband added, "I think so too."

Well, I wasn't the Davidsons' goddam financial advisor. "Okay, both of you take a trip out to this land development of his," I urged them. "If he takes you to the cleaners, but good, don't blame Donna and me for not warning you ahead of time." I turned to Jim. "Who do you think's paying for that altogether charming round of drinks Randolph bought us when he sat down? Do you think it's that son of a bitch? They'll be on *our* bill, you can bet on that. The next time you see him, if either of you are foolish enough to see him again, he'll apologize for completely forgetting the bar-bill when he left."

At Archie's funeral, after they'd lowered the expensive casket into the grave in the Randolph family plot, the seven or eight non-family mourners bagan drifting back to their cars across the wet white-covered

77

ground. I walked over to a patrician-looking old lady leaning on a heavy cane, and supported also by a middle-aged woman with Archie's weak chin and petulant mouth.

After I introduced myself the younger woman said, "This is our mother, and I'm Eva, Archibald's sister."

"I'm so pleased you're still enjoying your health, Mrs. Randolph," I said to the old lady.

She thanked me then said, "I didn't expect to outlive either of my children." After wiping her eyes she went on. "I'm rather hurt and surprised that so few of Archibald's old friends came to the funeral, or to the funeral home either for that matter. He'd been so good to so many of them, you know. A few years ago I cut off the few dollars a week I gave him, for he was in turn giving most of it away to men who were unemployed and so on."

I nodded, thinking that Archie had conned his own mother perhaps more than he had anyone else. I turned to Archie's sister and asked, "What was the cause of your brother's death, Mrs. — ?"

"*Miss* Randolph."

"I'm sorry."

"He took ill some months ago, developed jaundice, and had to be finally admitted to hospital. He passed away, the doctors told us, from cirrhosis of the liver. That was strange because he was never really drunk in his life, though he drank more on occasion than he should."

I nodded, through politeness not agreement.

With Eva and me holding the old lady under the arms we made our slow way across the sago-covered lawn to the undertaker's limousine. After placing Mrs. Randolph in the back seat of the car she said, "Archibald was such a lovely little boy, you know. He was always polite and charming with everyone he met."

"Yes he was," I said, thinking, even when he had his hand in their wallets.

"Thank you very much for coming," Mrs. Randolph said.

"Not at all, ma'am."

I bid the two women goodbye, and walked down the road to where my car was parked.

THE PREDESTINED DEATH OF SAMUEL GLOVER

It's been nothing but questions all day at the office. Every few minutes one of the other draftsmen would come over to my board and ask me about Sam's death. "What happened last night? Were you with him? Did it knock him down? Run over him? How'd he look? Was there much blood?"

They have no idea what it's like seeing a friend get killed like that, and having to answer all the questions by the police, the taxi company lawyer, and then by the fellows at work the next day. I'm going to tell it once more, the whole damn thing, and then I'm through.

Every night at five o'clock for the past seven or eight years Sam Glover and I have taken the elevator together, going home. Sam would buy his evening paper in the lobby, and then we'd walk up the street as far as Bloor where we separated, Sam to take a westbound subway train and I to take a northbound bus.

It had become an ingrained habit, this three-block walk, and I enjoyed it because Sam was an interesting old fellow to talk to. He was a bachelor who lived with a married sister away out in the west end of town. From some of the things he had told me on these short walks I'd learned that he was a believer in things like fate and premeditation. It was his favorite subject, and sometimes he'd point to people who passed us on the street and say, "There goes a man in a hurry to meet his fate," or, "He wants to reach his rendezvous, that one."

When I'd laugh, he'd say, "You'll find out some day that it's no joke. I've seen it happen. Every man is predestined to meet his death at a time and place already chosen, my boy."

I'd laugh and shake my head.

It was about three years ago that Sam told me where he was going to die. We were waiting for the lights to change at the Moulton Avenue intersection, when Sam said, "This is the place where fate is going to catch up to me."

I looked down at him and laughed, thinking he was joking. He was the type of mousey little man who would joke like that — or murder and dismember a victim.

"You may laugh, son, but it's true," he asserted in the good-natured, yet serious, way he had.

"Do you mean to tell me that you're going to be killed on this very corner?" I asked.

"That's right," he answered soberly.

When the lights changed, we crossed the street. I said to Sam, "If you know you're going to be killed here, why do you take this way home? You could walk to another subway station if you wanted to."

"It wouldn't be much use trying to avoid it," he answered. "Some day I'd forget, or have some business to transact along here — "

"Well, suppose you decided not to die at all. You could move to another town and live forever."

"Nobody lives forever," he answered patiently. "You can't avoid your fate. This is where it will happen, and nothing I can do will prevent it. I'm just hoping that it won't be for some time yet." He looked up at me and smiled apologetically, but I could see that he meant every word.

After that I brought the subject up occasionally as we were crossing Moulton Avenue, kidding him about being short-sighted, and about getting killed before his time if he wasn't careful. He would only smile at me and say, "You wait and see."

Last night we left the office as usual, about two minutes to five, in order to beat the rush to the elevators. Sam bought his paper in the lobby, and we emerged into the street.

As we brushed through the five o'clock crowd I asked Sam how his cat-cracker drawings for the Joyhills Refinery were coming along, and he told me he expected to finish them in a week; he was only waiting for some new tank specifications from McGuire, one of the engineers.

Looking up into the blue sky above the buildings I said, "It's going to be a nice evening. A change from the rain we've been having."

"Yes, it is. I'm going to do a little lawn bowling tonight," he answered. "It'll be my first chance this year. The greens have been a mess up to now."

When we reached the corner of Moulton the lights were still in our favor and we began to follow the crowd across the intersection. The lights changed from green to amber when we were halfway across, but we still had plenty of time. Old Sam stuck close to me as he always did. I saw this taxi cut around the stopped traffic and begin to cross the intersection as soon as it got the green light, so I shouted to Sam, and ran the last few yards to the opposite sidewalk.

I looked around just in time to see the taxi pick him up and throw him with a sickening plop against a hydrant about ten feet from the corner. There was the scream of the taxi's brakes and a lot of yelling from pedestrians.

By the time I reached Sam's side two men had laid him out on the sidewalk. Everbody was crowding aroung to get a better look at him. He was dead, of course, One side of his head was squashed like the soft spot on an orange.

A police car appeared from nowhere, and a policeman butted his way through the crowd, and asked what had happened. The cab driver came over from his taxi and told the policeman that he hadn't had a chance, this old man had run right in front of his cab. He seemed to be a nice young guy, who acted as if he wanted us all to believe him. I told the policeman I'd seen the accident. I tried to assure both him and the taxi driver that it hadn't been the driver's fault.

The taxi company's lawyer came to my house later last evening and questioned me about the accident. "I can't understand why your friend, Mr. Glover, would turn around and begin running the other way," he kept on saying.

"I've told you it wasn't your driver's fault, so why do you keep asking me questions like that?"

"Okay. I'm only trying to dope this thing out in case they have an inquest," he said.

If they have an inquest, I'm going to tell the same story I've just told here. I've been thinking it over and I'm sure Sam would have wanted it that way.

I heard the voice that told him to run back, but though the words came out of my mouth they weren't mine. Maybe I was predestined to prove Sam was right about fate killing him on that corner. Anyone else can call it what they like, but it wasn't I who killed Sam Glover.

82

JACKS OR BETTER, JOKERS WILD

After Swifty had gone there were only five of us left in my place: Lord Alfred and Harry McIntyre, young Jack Steepler and a girl who'd come in about nine, and myself behind the bar. I could see by the old Black Horse Ale clock on the back wall that closing time was less than an hour away. Lord Alfred, our dipso-in-residence, used to claim that the longest hour of the day was the one while he was waiting for the liquor store to open, but I've always thought it was the last one before mandatory closing time.

It was one of those evenings in the late fall when I was glad of my cardigan whenever the front door was opened. Not that it had opened much that night, it being Wednesday and the day before payday at the plant. Like my old Black Horse clock, which was two tin hands circling over a china pasture holding a dappled mare and colt, the plant itself was also becoming an antique, its payroll less than half what it once was, the diggings running out, and the machinery creaking its way to the scrap heap.

When I'd bought the tavern from Daley's widow, after I'd retired from Niagara Cement, the clock's mare and colt had been jet black and the limestone pits as white as spring trilliums. Age had dappled the horses on the clock and grayed the quarry walls, slaking sheds and kilns on the lip of the pits. The town of Limestone had shrunk to a village and Black Horse ale had shrunk to a nostalgic memory, as Lord Alfred might have put it.

I walked through the serving gate of the bar and picked up Swifty's two empty draft glasses and wiped the table. Old Harry McIntyre in the corner was holding his usual whispered conversation with his snub bottle of lager, giving somebody hell about his rights to ownership of a snake fence at the bottom of his farm. Harry and I had relived his whole life through many a slack winter afternoon, him arguing with his former wife Louise and just about everybody else you could think of, while I and his bottle listened quietly.

Ben Steepler's son Jack was sitting with the girl he'd introduced to me as Judy form the American Falls at a table under the front window. At first they'd been holding hands on top of the table but after about four bottles of ale apiece she was kept busy keeping Jack's hand away from her knee under it. Since they lowered the legal drinking age to eighteen there's been nights, after high school basketball games and dances, when *The Bear And Cub* seemed to be full of teenagers, whether they could prove their age or not: kids from Queenston, the Falls, St. Catherines and across the river in Lewiston and even as far away as Lockport.

Here on the Canada-U.S. border there's always been a friendly interchange of Canadians and Americans back and forth across the line, some of them working in one country and living in the other and families divided by the river. Most nights during the summer when the tourist business is good I'd have Sid Kirk serving table while I stuck strictly to the bar. We didn't get any of the mink stole crowd from the Shaw Festival at Niagara-on-the-Lake, but we *did* get the occasional actors, mainly English, who would come to the bar and order "a pint," as they always called it, to drink away from the autograph hounds.

Lord Alfred got along good with the theatricals, sometimes being invited to their tables or them joining him at his. Not that he was a real lord, though his accent sounded like it. As close to any members of the nobility I'm likely to get in this place are the pit foremen at lunchtime or Ollie Olander the slaking boss from the cement plant. There'd been a rumor going around here since Lord Alfred had settled in Limestone twenty years ago that he'd been an Imperial Army major who'd deserted his unit in Singapore during the war. It had gone on so long without any denial from Lord Alfred that I'd come to believe it myself. But as Sid Kirk, a former sergeant in The Lincoln and Welland Regiment, had once said, "What the hell does it matter any more anyways?"

I'd found out from Maggie Webster at the Queenston post office that Lord Alfred's real name was John Alfred Moore-Sheppard, and that he received two letters from England every month, one from the British government and the other from a firm called Sheppard Cutlery & Utensils in Derby, both of them containing cheques. The cutlery company cheques must have been his main income, for a wartime major's pension from the British army isn't enough to keep body and soul together even in Limestone. His government cheque should have been proof enough to me that he hadn't been cashiered or deserted, but I didn't really think of it.

When Elsie Daley and I were arranging the buying and selling of *The Bear And Cub* I'd kind of hinted to O'Donnell the manager of the bank in Queenston to give me a bit of information about Lord Alfred, but O'Donnell, who wouldn't give out the right time at less than ten-and-a-half percent, had answered with a mumbled profundity that sounded something like "That comes under the heading of financial privilege, Mr. Coates."

Well, on the particular night I'm talking about, Lord Alfred was seated at his usual four p.m. to midnight table against the wall opposite the bar, and far enough from old Harry not to be drawn in as a listener to Harry's rambling oral biography. His routine hardly ever varied after the Shaw Festival and the tourist season were over; he'd sit there over draft ales reading the Toronto evening paper from cover to cover, holding up one finger for his empty glass to be replaced, giving me a polite thank you each time it was, and otherwise appearing to be completely removed from his surroundings. Besides being quietly pleasant he could not only hold his drinks but could also hold his drunkenness, which is much harder to do. In the twenty years I'd been coming to the tavern, first as a patron and then as the owner of *The Bear And Cub*, I couldn't swear I'd ever seen Lord Alfred drunk, though I'd watched him coming and going, and knew for sure that he was.

I'd no sooner reached my place behind the bar again when the front door flew open and three men staggered in. I say staggered because they were just drunk and ornery enough to want to show they were. I made sure my junior size baseball bat was there under the cash register. They stood in indecision inside the door, looking over the place while the trio's leader, whom I didn't yet recognize as Ram McCauley, spread his mouth in a malicious thin-lipped grin. If they were waiting for a *maître d'* to show them to a table they were wasting their time.

Following the leader, a bigger and older man in khaki coveralls and a peaked cap, they finally sat down at a table, between Harry McIntyre and Lord Alfred but in the middle of the room. I walked over to take their orders.

"Got any 'Club?" one of the drunken young guys asked, forgetting which side of the river he was on I suppose. He was wearing an open green car coat over a dirty wool plaid shirt and his face was gaunt and looked pimpled whether it was or not. His hair was cut too long for my generation but too short for his own.

"No, sir. Just Canadian ales and lagers," I answered him.

"Gimme a Molson's Ex," the second young guy ordered. He was fatter than his partner and was wearing a G.I. jacket with the insignia ripped off, over a pair of U.S. army fatigues.

"I'll have the same, Coates," said the huge older man. When he spoke and called me by my name I recognized him as Ramsay Mc-Cauley who'd once worked a spell at the cement company when I was paymaster there.

"How's tricks, Ram?" I asked him.

"*I'm* doing all right. Been working at DuPont for fifteen years," he answered sourly. His shortened first name "Ram" hadn't come from his football days; he'd been called that when he was mucking in the limestone pit, and it fitted him. He was fatter now, maybe two-fifty, and as mean as I remembered him.

I brought back their drinks, and they nattered a bit about today's prices, especially on this side of the river, but Ram bought the round. When I was making change Ram asked, "How come you're working here, Coates?"

I told him about buying the place from Mrs. Daley five or six years before.

"You retired from the plant?"

"Yep. Where do you locate yourself now, Ram?"

"In the American Falls. This is my oldest boy, Vic," he said, pointing to the one in the army jacket.

"Hy, Vic."

No answer or even a look.

"The thin one's Eddie," Ram said.

This time neither Eddie nor I bothered greeting one another.

When I got back behind the bar and shut off the hot-dog rotiserrie I glanced over at the young couple under the window and saw that the girl looked scared and was tugging at Jack Steepler's sleeve.

I moved a couple of cases of empties out to the back and put the leftover sandwiches into the icebox. The next time I straightened up and looked around the tables I saw Ram McCauley hand a fifth of bourbon to the guy called Eddie, who took a good shot of it before passing it on to Vic and washing it down with ale. They were drinking boilermakers made up of Old Grandad and beer. I wasn't worried about them being spotted by a provincial inspector, not at that time of night, but I caught a whiff of trouble coming. I pulled my baseball bat pacifier out to the edge of the shelf.

The McCauleys and their friend were staring at Harry McIntyre, who was really giving hell to somebody represented by his empty bottle.

"Shut up, you crazy old bastard!" Vic McCauley shouted.

The other two laughed nastily at old Harry.

When they turned to their own table again Ram shouted at me, "Why'n the fuck you let that looney in here for, Coates!"

"He don't bother nobody," I answered, slipping into their argot. I moved along the back of the bar towards the cash register and my baseball bat. Jack Steepler and the girl were pretending not to have heard anything, and Lord Alfred was deep into his newspaper.

The skinny guy called Eddie said to me, "What kind of a fuckin bar d'ya call this anyways?"

I picked up my bat and let it swing from my right hand, hidden behind the bar. The three passed the Old Grandad around again. It was nearly empty, and Ram threw the paper bag it had come in on to the floor.

Now Eddie was staring at Jack Steepler and the girl. His stare was vicious like a cornered rat's. He shouted to her, "Did you think I wouldn't find you on this side of the river, Judy? Anyways what ya doin here with that creep?"

Judy grabbed Jack's arm, and though she whispered it I know she was begging him to take her out of the place. Jack Steepler shook his head.

"Wanna come home with us, Judy?" the skinny-faced Eddie asked, showing his brown teeth in a dirty leer.

Judy ignored him, staring desperately at Jack.

"We'll give ya a gang-bang on the River Road, Judy."

Ram McCauley snickered and poked his son in the ribs with a fat elbow. "Ask fer it in Chinee talk, Vic," he said. "Like ya did in Danang."

"You guys shut your mouths or hit the road!" I shouted.

"Aw shut up!"

I lifted the baseball bat so they could see it, and banged it on the top of the bar. Through the corner of my eye I saw Jack Steepler jump up from his chair and cover the zig-zag ten yards to where the three men were sitting. Even under his sport jacket you could notice his heavy chest and shoulders and his biceps straining the cloth of his upper sleeves. Running a power loader in the limestone quarry is a great muscle builder.

The McCauleys and their friend stood up.

Without a pause in his stride, and almost before Eddie could get his hands up, Jack Steepler decked him with a punch to the mouth. He fell back against an empty table which toppled chairs and screeched its way into the table behind it. He just lay there on the floor, out cold as a witch's tit.

Ram McCauley grabbed Jack and hollered, "How'd you like to try me, you young son of a bitch!"

"Yeah, both of us," his son Vic chimed in.

Jack broke away from McCauley and stepped back. Speaking to Ram he said, "Not you, you poor old bag of lard." Turning to the son he invited him, "Do as your daddy told you; ask Judy for it in Nam talk! Come on, ask her!"

As I swung through the serving gate with my baseball bat I caught a glimpse of Lord Alfred, his paper lowered to the table, laughing heartily to himself. I was too busy though to marvel at it at the time.

Vic McCauley made a lunge at Steepler, and young Jack stepped aside, grabbed the half-uniformed McCauley by the hair and jammed his face down on a table. By this time I was standing behind him with my persuader.

"You stay out of it, Coates," Ram said to me.

"Stay out of it hell!" I answered. "I own this joint!"

The older McCauley reached for the almost empty Old Grandad bottle, but I beat him to it. "Maybe you should have bought a fifth of Jack Daniels," I said. "A pair of jacks might have beaten one of a kind."

It took Steepler a couple of more smashes to Vic McCauley's face followed by three deep punches to his mid-section before McCauley backed away, pulling a handkerchief from his pocket and dabbing at his nose.

"All right, it's closing time," I said. I walked over and pulled old Harry McIntyre to his feet and steered him in the direction of the front door. As I turned around again, so help me God, there was Lord Alfred with a finger upraised for another draft. "Bloody good show!" he shouted.

As if noticing Lord Alfred for the first time old McCauley shouted, "Close your trap, you Limey bastard. I heard all about you deserting in Burma or someplace. I served in the U.S. Marines and my boy there fought in the Nam!"

"The U.S. Marines were good," said Lord Alfred, "but it depended where you served, didn't it?" His accent always reminded me of the Queen reading her Christmas message.

"Time I closed," I said to Lord Alfred as I headed back to the bar.

"Yes, Mr. Coates. See you tomorrow," he said. Something in him had changed though, and his narrowed eyes were enough to scare you. Without another word the little Englishman folded his newspaper and left by the front door.

It took both McCauleys a couple of minutes to bring their friend Eddie around, then the three of them sat down again at their table and finished their beer between threatening glances in my direction. Steepler and the girl left, and I heard their car driving out of the parking lot. I picked up the phone and dialed my house at the northern limits of Niagara Falls. My wife Madge answered, and I told her, "I'm closing up soon, dear. Keep your ear to the phone until I talk to you again. If you hear anything strange, or I tell you to, call Niagara Region Police and send them to *The Bear And Cub*."

"You phoning the fuzz?" young McCauley asked sarcastically.

"No, my wife."

"Maybe we should wipe that fucking bar with you," Ram McCauley threatened.

"You do and my wife will call the police and you'll be stopped before you make any of the bridges." I placed the telephone receiver on top of the bar.

When they left, after peevishly sweeping the bottles and glasses from their table to the floor, Ram McCauley promised over his shoulder, "Maybe I'll bring some of the boys over from the Veterans of Foreign Wars post in the U.S. Falls and clean out this joint."

"Make it tomorrow night," I said. "And make sure the veterans are real ones and not guys like you who stayed Stateside as a drill instructor at Camp Lejeune, North Carolina."

Ram slammed the door hard enough to rattle every glass in the tavern.

After I'd bolted the door, I told my wife everything was okay now and she could hang up. Maybe I shouldn't have thrown Ram McCauley's chicken shit war service in his face like that. As Sid Kirk had said about Lord Alfred, "What the hell does it matter any more anyways?"

The Bear And Cub is only about 300 yards from the River Road along the Canadian side of the Niagara Gorge, but out of sight of the gorge due to a large clump of trees and a sharp curve in the Limestone Sideroad. By the time I reached the River Road that night the narrow highway was blocked with cars, two or three of them belonging to both the Ontario Provincial Police and the Niagara Regional Police, their dome lights flashing red in the darkness. I parked off the Limestone Sideroad and ran forward to see what had happened. Somebody told me that a car bearing New York licence plates had swung off the Limestone Road, had blown a tire, and had plunged through the guard rail and down the sheer cliff into the river many yards below. I knew even before I was told that the car was the one driven by Ram McCauley.

I introduced myself to the police on the scene, and a few minutes later a senior officer in plain clothes arrived and questioned me more closely. By the time the police and some of the stopped motorists had searched the cliffside with the help of powerful searchlights on tow trucks drawn up to the ragged hole in the guard rail, without finding any survivors, bodies or the car itself, the plainclothes officer asked me to follow him in his car to police headquarters in Niagara Falls. He also asked the first person on the scene, a man who was driving from Chippawa to Queenston, and had seen the car swerve through the guardrail into the river, to come along too.

At police headquarters the man who had seen the accident insisted that he had heard a blowout just before the car swerved into the guardrail and disappeared over the cliff. I told the police that if it had been the McCauley car that had run off the road I would have to blame the accident on the driver's drunkenness, no matter which one of the three had been driving. I was asked who else had been in *The*

Bear and Cub that evening, and I gave them the names of Jack Steepler and his girl Judy, Lord Alfred and old Harry McIntyre.

When the McCauley car failed to return to the American side of the river the New York State Police had followed the drunken trail left by the McCauleys and Eddie from bar to bar, to liquor store, American Legion post, and finally to the international bridge at Lewiston. Ram McCauley had been driving an old convertible, which because of the chilly night had had its roof up. By the following evening the police on both sides of the border, and the press, were convinced that the car had indeed been Ram McCauley's.

Lord Alfred and Harry McIntyre both turned up at *The Bear And Cub* after being questioned by the police. Old Harry hadn't been able to tell them much, but Lord Alfred had corroborated my evidence about the drunkenness of the car's occupants. Jack Steepler had an alibi as to the time he'd crossed into Niagara Falls, New York, and also the early morning hour when he had returned after driving the girl Judy home, from both the U.S. and Canadian immigration and customs officers.

It took the U.S. Coastguard from Youngstown and some Ontario Provincial Police frogmen several days to find the wreck of the convertible in the fast icy currents of the Niagara River, and a couple of days after that before the car was brought to the surface by a heavy crane brought down from the Welland Canal. Apparently the convertible's cloth roof had been ripped off during its tumble down the cliff, and none of the bodies had been found.

One afternoon during the spring following the McCauley's accident I took Lord Alfred his glass of ale, and he showed me a short item in the Toronto paper about the two young men's decomposed bodies being washed ashore off Niagara-on-the-Lake.

"I don't feel any sorrow for them, Major," I said. "They had it coming to them."

"*De mortuis nil nisi bonum*, Mr. Coates."

"What does that mean?"

"Loosely translated from Latin, Mr. Coates, I suppose it means, 'Speak no ill of the dead.' I've seen too many young men killed in my lifetime, and though they both deserved the drubbing that young man — what's his name? — yes, Jack Steepler gave them, it was too bad they had to die."

That was one of the last times I ever talked to Lord Alfred I guess. Before the month was out he too had died, of pneumonia, in a Niagara Falls hospital.

Strangely, on the same day Lord Alfred died, they found a badly decomposed body washed up on the beach at Port Dalhousie. The body was identified as Ramsay McCauley's from his dental plates. The pathologist who carried out the forensic autopsy on Ram McCauley believed that his death had not been caused by either the car accident or by drowning, but by a high-powered bullet through his skull.

Last summer when the George Bernard Shaw Festival presented *Candida* I looked up one afternoon to find myself facing a young English couple, who asked me for "two pints please," and then carried them from the bar to an empty table. Later the man called me from the bar and introduced himself as William Shakleton and his wife as Doris Delane, who played the title role in the play.

Mr. Shakleton asked me if I was familiar with Jack Moore-Sheppard who was believed by them to live in the neighborhood. It took me a moment to realize he was talking about Lord Alfred.

"I *did* know him," I said. "He came in here every day but Sunday for twenty years."

"He's stopped coming here?" Mr. Shakleton asked.

"He died in April," I told them.

The young couple stared at each other.

"Hard lines, Bill," the wife said. "I knew how much you were looking forward to meeting Joker, if not for your sake then for your father's."

"Joker?" I asked.

"It was his *nom de guerre* out in Malaysia and Siam during the war," the husband said.

"Just a moment please." I hurried to the bar and brought back three draft ales. "It's on the house," I said. "Please tell me about Joker?"

"There isn't a great deal to tell," Mr. Shakelton said. I began to hate the English for their reticence and habit of understatement.

"Please go on."

"You knew his name I suppose. Major John Alfred Moore-Sheppard,

Retired, D.S.O. and bar, M.C. and bar, etcetera, etcetera?"

"I didn't know anything about his decorations."

"Well, to make a long story short, old man, he was taken prisoner when the Japanese overran Singapore. He subsequently escaped and became the leader of a small band of Malay and Chinese partisans working behind the Japanese lines. Blowing up trains, bridges, ambushing and assassinating high Jananese officers, that sort of thing. He finally made radio contact with Calcutta, and was given many hazardous assignments by Allied intelligence. He was one of the very few to escape from a Japanese prison camp and live to tell about it — "

"But he didn't tell about it. Not around here anyway."

"Quite. He wouldn't of course. My father was with intelligence in Calcutta and later Burma, and was actually the one who gave Major Moore-Sheppard his code name of Joker. At one time the enemy set a price on his head of half a million Malay dollars. He and his men were supplied by air-drops by the R.A.F. and the Americans, unfortunately most of which were aborted by the enemy. It must have been a hell of a life, moving through the jungle every day to escape enemy patrols and even the local populace who would have given him up for the reward. He was eventually captured again and tortured."

"How?"

"Let's just say he came back to England after his release no longer a real man. That's what brought him to Canada and to this — pardon me, Mr. Coates — out-of-the-way place."

"He turned down a knighthood, didn't he, Bill?" the wife asked.

"Yes. I think though that what he hated to give up most was his marksmanship. Before the war he'd been one of the top riflemen of the British Bisley Team."

"We used to call him Lord Alfred — because of his accent," I said, suddenly ashamed of the name we'd given him. "I — I suppose it was his — condition that kept him to himself and made him drink every day?"

"I would think so." After a moment Mr. Shakleton asked, "By any chance did you know where he lived?"

"In the last house down the road towards the river. It's not too far. Just a small cottage, what we call here a shack."

"Alone?"

"Yes. Always alone. His only social life as far as I ever knew was sitting in here and reading the Toronto paper."

"How did he die, Mr. Coates?"

"Pneumonia. The banker down in Queenston, Mr. O'Donnell, handled his affairs. I think his remains were shipped back to Derbyshire."

"Yes. He and his brother had inherited a small manufacturing concern in Derby I believe."

I excused myself to serve some customers, and when I was finished I found the Shakletons had gone. They never returned to *The Bear And Cub*.

The following morning I walked along the Limestone Sideroad past the shanty occupied for so long by Lord Alfred. I noticed that he'd had a perfect line of fire from his east window to the intersection of the sideroad and the River Road. To a man of his skill with a rifle it would have been nothing at all to have picked off Ram McCauley at the wheel of the old convertible, and remembering his eyes when he'd left the tavern that night it seemed not only possible but probable that he had. Though the police had searched our houses for firearms after the accident, especially Lord Alfred's, they'd found nothing. Of course getting rid of a rifle and ammunition here on the Niagara Gorge is as easy as merely throwing it over a sheer cliff into a tenknot current.

I'll let Major John Alfred Moore-Sheppard, Retired, D.S.O. and bar, M.C. and bar, etcetera, etcetera, remain as a fading memory under his anonymity as dipso-in-residence at *The Bear And Cub*. What was the Latin phrase he'd quoted to me? 'Speak no ill of the dead.'

Though the witness who had viewed the accident had sworn he'd heard a blowout just before the accident, when the car was recovered from the river all its tires were found to be intact.

THE CUSTOMER IS ALWAYS RIGHT

Down at our service station there were always a couple of guys who dropped in to chew the fat with Red and myself. It seemed that this was a throwback to the days when the old livery stable was the hangout for the men of the town. Before Eddie Moffat was married, and was still going to technical school, he was one of them. Sometimes these hangers-out used to be a nuisance, but Eddie never was; he'd never ask foolish questions or get in the way of Red or me when we were working on a job.

Now that few people were buying new cars we had plenty of repair work to do on their old ones, and believe me some of them were real clinkers.

After Eddie Moffat married young Eileen McMaster he came around less often than when he was single. He had a couple of little jobs after he was married: an assistant butcher down at the A&P and for a while he worked an extra crew at the post office, but he quit or lost them both. Finally after young Steve Wardell quit the station to go to a community college I gave Eddie his job of running my pumps.

Eddie was a good worker actually, not too bright but friendly and helpful to the customers, and my regulars all liked him. Lately though something had been bothering him, and I wondered what it was. Not that he'd ever volunteer any information, but he seemed sort of distracted and worried about something. Red, who lived on the same street as Eddie and his wife told me once he thought it had to do with Eileen's boss Bill Johnson. Since Johnson had sold his old man's farm for a bundle of dough to a development outfit he'd bought himself a wardrobe of clothes that were too young for him, let his sideburns grow, and pictured himself as a swinger, though he was nearly my age. He'd also bought a franchise in one of those cheap "steak" houses where they served a slab of fried beef, a baked potato, a hot biscuit and butter, and one of those salads that are all chopped lettuce with a slice of tomato on top.

Eddie's wife Eileen worked as a waitress in Johnson's joint, and though Red couldn't prove anything he'd seen Johnson driving Eileen home late at night quite often. Don't get me wrong, Eileen is a nice kid, but sometimes the attention of an older man like Johnson goes to a young girl's head, even though he was probably as useless as tits on a nun to any woman in bed. Though we didn't talk much about it

Johnson's obvious play for Eddie's young wife bothered both Red and me. Both of us had attended the Moffat wedding down at St. Luke's, and we sort of took a sort of uncles' interest in the kids.

As Red said to me one day, "You know, Joe, there's times when I feel like asking young Eddie what's eating him. Like I used to take my own kids on my knee on ask them to tell me where it hurts." That's the same way I felt about it, but hell you can't ask a man twenty-two years old that sort of thing.

Bill Johnson, although he's been a regular customer of mine since I opened the gas station nearly twenty years ago, has always been a surly kind of jasper who'd kick about his repair bills, worry us silly when we were giving him a tune-up or rotating his tires, and generally make himself a nuisance around the station. Hell, I remember him before his old man died and he sold the farm when he used to drive a second-hand Dodge. When he moved up to the Kiwanis Club and began to call himself a businessman he became even worse, and when he bought himself the Cadillac he'd stand in the bay watching us work on it, as if we were fly-by-night crooks ready to make off with his wheel-covers.

He was always snotty too to young Eddie Moffat when he'd stop in for gas, and Red and I didn't like that either. He'd make Eddie wash both his windshield and his rear window. Once he came steaming into my office to complain that Eddie had left a greasy handprint on his fender, and I told him to take his bloody heap down to the car wash two blocks away, and not bother me with that kind of complaint.

It was early last March when Johnson brought his car in to have its annual overhall. He insisted we put it on the lift right away, though I pointed to the lot full of cars that had priority, including a Pontiac that had to be fitted with new shocks and ball joints and a Galaxy that needed pinion and ring gears. He insisted that he needed the job done right away. Because he'd been a regular customer so long I gave in that time, and we put his car into one of the bays. We gave him an oil change, new oil and gas filters, and a lube job. He'd brought along a pair of regular tires in his trunk, and he wanted us to take off his winter tires and put them on in their place.

It had rained all night, and the radio had called for a drop in temperature that morning. I told Johnson that he was crazy to change his tires yet, that we might still be in for some snow. No, he wanted the tires changed right there and then. Our motto at Broadway Esso has always been "The customer is always right!" Stupid maybe, but right, you know what I mean?

After we'd backed his car out of the bay, Johnson asked either Red or me to take the car for a spin, and I told him no way. I told him we had enough work to keep us both working overtime that night, his car was running like a Swiss watch, and neither of us was taking him on a Mickey Mouse spin. "How about this guy," he said, pointing to young Eddie. He didn't even have the courtesy to call the kid by his name, though he knew it as well as anybody.

"Listen, Johnson," I told him. "From now on I don't want your business. Take this high-priced heap back to your dealer's for servicing or go down the street to the Gulf or Shell stations. I've taken enough of your Kiwanis-businessman's crap to last me a lifetime."

"You've got to take me for a test drive," he said. "Isn't that procedure after you've done a tune-up?"

"Only to somebody like you," I told him. "And don't tell me anything about procedure; I've been in this business long enough to know more about mechanic's procedure than you'll ever know."

"Well then, how about sending this guy along," he said, pointing to young Eddie. "He's a yo-yo, but I suppose he can drive a car?" This was all said within Eddie's hearing, but the kid didn't even crack a frown.

"Okay, Johnson, I'll send Eddie with you. He'll drive, and you can strain your ears to catch any noises of mechanical errors. If you hear anything you don't like, and it's our fault, we'll adjust it free of charge. Eddie knows what he's doing."

Eddie climbed into Johnson's car and buckled his seat belt.

"What the hell you want to wear a seat belt for? You chicken or something?" Johnson asked him.

I said, "Any of my employees that drives a car out of here wears a seat belt; it's one of my rules. If you don't like it, Johnson, the kid doesn't drive your car, okay?"

Johnson didn't say anything, for if he had I'd have pulled Eddie out of the car there and then. Johnson didn't buckle up, being one of those smartypants who think wearing a seat belt is not masculine or something.

I said to Eddie, "Take the car along Eglinton and work the brakes at every stop light. Then put her full out down the Parkway. If you're picked up for exceeding the speed limit don't let it worry you; Johnson can afford any speeding tickets. Now the roads are pretty treacherous right now, Eddie, so watch it. There's ice forming in places, and it's just thin enough to fool a driver."

"Okay, McIver," Johnson said. "Are you sure you don't want to give this kid his bottle before we leave? He's useless enough without you babying him. As it is he makes young Eileen go to work to help support him."

Eddie Moffat didn't say anything, but I could sense the hate he felt for Johnson. There was something too about the way Johnson had mentioned Eileen Moffat by her first name, not calling her "his wife" but Eileen, as if he was bragging to the kid about being intimate with his wife. I'm only a gas-station stiff, not a psychologist, but I figured there might be more going on between Johnson and young Eileen than either Red or I had guessed up to that time.

As they drove down the street Red and I watched them go.

"I think young Eddie's going to give Johnson the ride of his life," Red said, laughing.

"I hope he scares the living shit out of him," I said.

We drove a sixty-nine Mustang on to the lift, then broke off for lunch, having to stop every now and then to gas up a car at the pumps.

It was about a half hour later when I got the phone call from the police. It was from a sergeant of the Traffic Division, who told me there'd been a fatal accident down on the Parkway near the Leaside Bridge. A Cadillac registered to William Johnson had gone out of control on a patch of glare ice and had plowed through the safety fence and into one of the bridge abutments.

"Who was killed?" I asked.

"William Johnson. He went right through the windshield. Christ, what a mess!"

"What about the driver, Eddie Moffat?"

"Luckily he was wearing a seat belt. We think he has a broken leg, but that's all. He's on his way to the hospital now."

"How about the car?"

"Practically totalled, or at least of couple of thousand dollars worth of damage to the front end."

I told the sergeant that Moffat was an employee of mine, and had been driving Johnson's car on a test run following a tune-up at my garage.

"We know. We got all that before they took Moffat to the hospital."

I told the sergeant that I'd warned Johnson about taking off his winter tires, and the sergeant told me they'd found them in the car trunk. He said, "The spot where the accident happened is pretty treacherous. We've been trying to get it sanded all morning. We had a minor accident in the same place during this morning's rush hour."

"Are there any charges being laid against young Moffat?"

"No, it was just one of those things," the sergeant said. "I don't think the driver even saw the ice. There wasn't any skid marks anyway. A big car like that just pushed the safety fence in like tissue paper, and split the front end of her open on the bridge abutment. We can't even tell what speed he was travelling at because the speedometer is all screwed up."

"Do you want me to get in touch with Mrs. Moffat or Mrs. Johnson?"

"No. That's already been taken care of," the sergeant said.

After the phone call Red and I sat in the office finishing our lunches.

"I can't say I'm sorry about that son of a bitch Johnson," Red said.

"Neither am I. Maybe I'd better find out how Eddie's doing though. I forgot to ask the police sergeant what hospital they took him to."

"It's too early yet anyway, Joe. You know I sort of had the feeling something like this was going to happen."

"I did too, Red. Between you and me I think I *knew* it was going to happen."

"You know, Joe, it's funny how a quiet young guy like Eddie will brood over something, never saying a word about it, and then get even somehow with the guy or the woman that's doing something to hurt him."

"Yeah, Red, it's funny all right."

"I guess we'd better get to work on that Mustang, Joe, or we're going to be working till midnight."

"Yeah, we'd better."

The bell rang as a car pulled up to the pumps.

"I'll get it," Red said. He got up and left the office.

I got on the phone and called a kid a couple of blocks away who sometimes helped on the pumps after school. He promised to come right over to give Red and me a hand. Then I phoned the Workmens' Compensation Board and reported Eddie's accident.

STATION BREAK

The floor director stood beside Camera Two and counted off the seconds with his fingers, mouthing them audibly, " . . . seven, six, five, four . . . . " At "one" the red light on Camera Two came on and Ricky Ellson, his professional smile already set, said, "Good evening, ladies and gentlemen, here is your eight hundred and fourth edition of What Gives?, your Thursday evening give-and-take between a distinguished panel of personalities in the news and– " A broad wink that for the 804th time received the homage of free-pass giggles from the studio audience. " – some who wish they were not." He flashed his mocking grin at the dimly illuminated faces of those in the front row of studio chairs.

"Tonight my panel guests are," said Ellson, turning his good profile to Camera Three and smiling, "a famous figure of the art world, Jeremy Cronitz – " A pause to allow the audience to obey the flashing AP-PLAUSE signs. " – Ms Mina Parelli, who will demonstrate, a little later, her fabulous line of Headkerchiefs – ?" A questioning pout to the Parelli woman, who nodded. " – Jim Branruff of The Miners football team who needs my introduction like he needs a raise in salary." Some female gigles and a guffaw or two from the TV football jocks in the back rows. "Peter Normande, well-known in our part of the country for his irascible comments, his refusal to hedge or compromise, and his digging for the truth on this area's most listened-to radio hot line." There was no need for the applause signs as the audience gave Normande an unstinting ovation.

Normande, a good-looking young Jew with his hair brushed across his ears like a sheepdog, smiled and nodded to various sections of the audience.

Ellson went on. "And last but certainly not the farthest to my left except on this occasion – " His voice rose habitually to a mild crescendo. "– the distinguished *litterateur*, Bellingham Turner."

The applause sign flashed frantically, the audience paid back more than its free-entry debt to the studio with its hands, and palms up to still the clapping, Ricky said, "And we'll all be back – " Patented thump of fist in palm. " – right after these messages."

Camera Three moved over to stage right and focussed on the audience, while Camera Two closed up on the panel at a word from the floor director. Camera One remained in its position at extreme stage left, its blind eye trained on the program credits cards set up on a wooden easel against the wall.

During the commercials there were instructions from Norman Peterson, the director, sitting in the control room out of sight of the studio, to Bob Grayling, the floor director.

Peterson said, "We're getting a shadow on the bottom right of the cards." The floor director told a gaffer to erase it with a light. *Peterson said, "That's better, Bob. We'll open with Two on Ellson and then swing across the whole panel. Ellson will open up with Cronitz, so you, Camera Three, pick up Cronitz and hold. Camera Two stays with Ellson for the time being. I want the name cards – and make sure they're straight; they drooped a little to the left during the run-down – flashed for sixty seconds below shoulder height. We'll take care of that up here. Everything else okay, Bob?"*

Bob Grayling said into his mike, "The Parelli woman is wearing her dress too high for the program's image and the shape of her gams."

"Tell her to pull it down. She's not demonstrating panty-hose but her babushkas or whatever she calls them."

Grayling walked over to the panel and asked Miss Parelli to pull her dress down an inch or two, if she didn't mind.

The little-girl voice of the script assistant, also in the control room, reading a stopwatch, came over the floor headsets, "Ten, nine, eight . . ."

Ellson said, "Ready, everybody. Remember this is a live program."

Jeremy Cronitz moved the carefully arranged disreputable knot of his bandana a trifle and leaned forward in his chair. At sixty Cronitz wore the polka dot bandana not as an arty habilment but to hide his turkey neck. Mina Parelli pulled her dress down a quarter of an inch, and stretched her arm along the back of her chair to emphazise her breasts, which were as inadequate as her legs. Bellingham Turner cast a world-weary eye at the dimly seen audience beyond the lights and raised his eyebrows a bit, giving himself his hoped-for TV image of an artistic, academic don who was merely fulfilling his publisher's and public's demand by being there. Peter Normande pulled some small note cards from his jacket pocket and palmed them in the clasped hands he held against his fancy waistcoat. Jim Branruff, the big football player, his handsome black face contorted into an amused grin, tried to squeeze himself down into the inadequate panelist's chair, gave it up and leaned forward with his hands on his knees.

As the red on-camera light lit up on Camera Two Rickey Ellson went into his professional breathless questioning of his guests. "Well, Mr. Cronitz, we'll start with you. Since your show of oils at the Homburg Gallery you've gone back to your first love, sculture. Your very interesting work, 'Pedestrian,' was unveiled last week in the courtyard of the Ethical Life Assurance Centre."

Cronitz nodded unsmilingly.

Ellson, who had been waiting expectantly for an answer, recovered and went on. He thought, my God, I've caught myself a dummy! "Your 'Pedestrian' has aroused quite a bit of public reaction." Glancing frantically at his notes. "Some of your fellow artists have called it a rip-off, and it's also been referred to in uncomplimentary terms by the critics and public."

"What they know about art?" Cronitz asked him in his thick Slavic accent.

"Well . . ." Ellson turned his professional grin at the camera. He could feel himself beginning to sweat.

Peter Normande saved the show from dying by saying, off camera, "One of the phone-ins on *my* show called it a twenty thousand dollar hallucination put together by a psychotic pipe-fitter."

Peterson, in the control room, told his switcher to get an audience reaction on Camera Three, and he cued Camera Two to move along the panel to the speaker. He said to Grayling, "Jeez, Bob, those cameras aren't immovable objects. See that Joe on Camera Two moves with the speakers. We lost Normande on that pipe-fitter sentence."

There wasn't a word from Cronitz, the other members of the panel, or Ellson. Peterson glanced up at the Camera Three monitor and saw that it was focussed on three of the ugliest-looking old biddies in the studio. He shouted into his mike, "Grayling, get those cameras moving! Cue Three to pan across the audience!"

Ricky Ellson recovered and asked, "Have you any answer to that, Mr. Cronitz?"

"To what?"

There were titters from the studio audience.

Peterson said, "Get off those cards Number One! Swing to the panel and try to beat Camera Two to the person we're getting the audio from. Stay on the panel." To Bob Grayling he said, "Cue Ellson to fill in those visual gaps. Tell him this is TV not radio."

There was a background crash in the studio as Camera One knocked over the easel and its painted credit cards as it swung to cover the panel. Bob Grayling waved his hands wildly as he sent a pair of grips to repair the damage.

Norm Peterson turned to the script girl, who was sitting beside him at the control panel with a stopwatch in her hand and one lying face up in front of her. "What in Christ's name was that!" He brushed his long hair over his eyes with his hand.

The girl shook her head, her eyes glued to the monitors.

Peterson flicked on his mike. "What in hell happened down there, Bob?"

"Camera One knocked down the card easel. I'm getting it looked after."

Tiredly, "Roger."

Ellson, now grasping at straws, forgot his on-camera voice and in a strained falsetto spoke across the silent panel to Bellingham Turner. "Mr. Turner, as a fellow artist, though not through the same medium as Mr. Cronitz, what do *you* think of his sculpture, 'Pedestrian'?"

Turner flashed his self-congratulatory smile at the studio audience, and ignoring Ellson spoke directly into Camera Two. From a small weak mouth made smaller by his mutton chop sideburns he said, "I haven't seen it. As a matter of fact I have yet to see the Ethical Life Centre either. I seldom go downtown, but usually send a secretary to conduct everyday business."

Ellson murmured a thanks to the Almighty as Peter Normande broke in. "You have a secretary, Bellingham? Just like the president of A.T. & T?"

Camera One, luckily, was on Normande, though Two had been a moment late swinging from Ellson to Turner. Peterson watched his control room monitors with dread. He turned to the script assistant and asked, "How long to the second commercial break, Sylvia?" She told him it was six minutes. The young switcher was still the coolest person in the control room, switching pictures and audio from one clip-on mike or camera to another as best he could and putting them on the air.

"I've been pleading with the front office to pre-tape this show for months," Peterson said, forgetting to cut off his voice from the floor crew. He heard a low laugh from one of the cameramen over his headset.

On the stage Turner answered Normande. "I have *two* secretaries, Mr. Normande. One for my academic work and the other for my literary avocation. Besides which I'd thank you not to use my Christian name so familiarly."

"Okay, Turner," Normande said, bending forward as if he were speaking into a radio desk mike, and glancing at the top card in his hand. "What did you think of the critics' reaction to your latest book, *Memoirs Of A Literary Man?* It seems to me they cut you up pretty good. The *Sun*'s book critic called it — and I quote — 'A literary pretension by an aging academic who should be stoned to death with marshmallows by this country's younger writers.'"

Turner gave a strained deprecatory grin towards Camera One, then finding it was not focussed on him, held it as he turned to Camera Two. "The *Sun*'s critic is a young copyist," he said in carefully enunciated academic English. "The 'stoned to death with marshmallows' line is a repeat of what a Florida newspaper columnist once said about the entertainer Liberace."

"Does that mean it wasn't apt then, Turner?" asked Normande.

"It was not apt but inept literary criticism from an illiterate newspaper book-reviewer."

Bob Grayling spoke into his mike to Peterson. "Shall we stay with them, Norm?"

Peterson answered, "If we don't we're dead. Thank God we've got Normande on the show. But cue Ellson to get in there now and then. After all, the show carries his name."

Grayling knelt down beside Camera One and caught Ricky's eye. He poked his finger several times towards his mouth. Ellson nodded.

Normande went on as if speaking to a loathsome caller on his phone-in radio show. "You're sort of a literary relic, Turner, you know. What have you ever *done* except wrap yourself in cotton-batten and

105

live out your nice-nelly life in the halls of Academe?"

Bellingham Turner, his mouth returned to its tiny slit once more, tried to butt in, as did Ricky Ellson, but Peter Normande went on remorselessly. Shuffling his note cards in his hand he said, "A few years ago you made the most asinine remark to an interviewer in the Herald that I've ever read." Glancing at his notes. "It was the issue of July ninth, nineteen-seventy. I made a note of it then, hoping that some day I'd have a chance to use it." He turned to Ellson then back to Turner sitting in the outermost chair.

Peterson said into his open mike, "Camera One get Turner's reaction. Hold on him for a few seconds. Camera Two get Ellson's face. Close up on him a little then swing back to Normande."

Normande said, "You told the *Herald* interviewer, Turner, that nobody should ever write for money. Remember?"

"Of course I remember," Turner said. "I'm not a vicious little disk jockey who has to make notes. I meant what I said too. To an artist, literary or not, the financial return from his art should be of secondary importance."

"It's easy for you to say, Turner. You've always had two, not one as you claim, avocations. The college bit has been one and writing novels has been another. Your father was always a wealthy man, the owner of a network of radio stations in the West and a tattletale gray eminence in this country's political life. When he died he left you a bundle, not that you ever needed it, so why in hell *shouldn't* money be secondary to you? But what about many of the writers who have had to depend on their craft — and are still doing it — to feed, clothe and house themselves or their families? To me, Bellingham, you're nothing but a phony dilettante!"

There was an unexpected burst of applause from the audience, which was made up largely of people living in flats, rooms and apartments in the city's downtown core. At this time of year, without the scattering of out-of-towners it contained in the summer, the studio crowd was also made up of the financially poor.

Norm Peterson flicked his mike switch and told Camera Two to get back to Ellson. He shouted, "Number One, for chrissakes pan slowly over the audience!"

Bob Grayling asked, "What about Turner?"

"Forget him! Cue Ellson to Jim Branruff. Camera Two, get a close-up of Ellson. Number One, finish your audience pan shot and get on Branruff and hold."

The script assistant said, "One minute to commercial break, Norm."

"Thanks, Sylvia." He flicked his switch and told the floor director and the cameramen, "That last interchange between Normande and Turner was fabulous TV. So was the audience reaction. Your pan shot was perfect, Number One."

A worried-looking Ellson came on the control room monitor from Camera Two. He was peering beyond the cameras.

Peterson held open his mike switch with a finger. "Bob, we've only got sixty seconds to commercial break. Sylvia will give you the countdown from ten. Get Ellson to say something witty, or outraged, or some fucking thing. Then count him down."

"I'm trying to get to him, but he's stunned or something."

"He's always been stunned. Did you ever know a talk show host who wasn't stunned? Except Johnny Carson and Dick Cavett? Start counting down."

The script assistant began, "Ten, nine, eight . . . . "

Bob Grayling began counting down with his finger.

During the commercial break Ricky Ellson took off his microphone and stepped over to Bob Grayling. "Let me talk to Peterson, Bob."

The floor director handed him his mike and headset.

"Norm, what the hell are you doing to me! This show's going to end up in a Donnybrook!"

"Keep it cool, Rick, baby. The last few minutes between Normande and Turner was real live TV. The studio audience reflected the viewing audience, I'm sure. Now, as soon as we're back on the air I'm putting Branruff on camera and you begin with him. Don't worry, this show's going to raise your ratings. What the hell do you want, a constant line-up of broads who've written nature food cookbooks, guys who are flogging 'best selling' novels that nobody's ever heard of, and smart-ass young actors who've hitchhiked home after playing a bit part in an off-Broadway porno? Don't worry, you won't have to go back to the real estate dodge tomorrow. Anyway it was you, not me, who wanted to put Turner and Normande on the same show. You didn't expect Normande to let that phony bastard get away with calling himself

'an artist' and 'a literary man', did you? Jesus, Rick, writers, unless they're phonies like Turner, would never use either of those terms about themselves."

Ellson, not wholly reassured, "Okay, Norm."

He gave the headset and mike back to the floor director and went back to his chair.

The script assistant began her countdown at the end of the commercials.

Peterson said into his mike, "You've got Camera Two on Ellson and Camera Three on Branruff, right, Bob?"

"Yep."

"What's Camera One doing? It should be on the name flashes. Don't forget sixty seconds of Branruff's name, below shoulder height, as soon as he's on camera."

"They're looking for his name card now, Norm."

"What!"

"The cards got mixed up when the easel was knocked over. There's a grip going through the cards now."

"All right, we'll hold off the cards until it's found. Start counting down with Sylvia now. When the card is found we'll give it a sixty-second flash."

The switcher put Ricky Ellson on camera and Ricky smiled into Camera Two and said, "Now I'd like to call on another of my guests whose name, I know, is more than familiar to everyone in my audience. That great Miners running back — " He smiled over at Jim Branruff.

The unmistakable Slavic accent of Jeremy Cronitz interrupted the introduction. "Me too, like Mr. Bellingham there, thinks money is the second t'ing. I — "

"Alex, cut him off!" Peterson cried to the switcher. "What the hell's that old pipe-fitter doing with an open mike anyway? Cut him off completely."

The switcher, his eyes on the monitors, flipped the audio switch connecting the network to Cronitz' neck microphone.

Ellson gave Cronitz a strained smile, then as if no interruption had occurred, said, "Ladies and gentlemen — " (A pause as his voice recovered its professional crescendo) " — Jim Branruff!"

There was a satisfying round of applause from the studio audience. Branruff smiled and nodded.

Ellson said, "It's certainly good to have you on the show, Jim. I don't think many of us will forget that final game of the regular season when you made that spectacular forty-five yard – you hear that, folks? – forty-five yard touchdown run against the Saints!"

Branruff cut into the applause. "I had some excellent running interference from Johnny Orlando and Steve Bennett," he said.

The name, JIM BRANRUFF, flashed a little too high on the screen but better late than never.

Ellson said, "I understand from the papers, Jim, that you're signed up for next season with the Miners offence?"

"That's right, Rick. That's why I'm in town right now."

"And we're all glad you are. Right, folks?"

"Heavy applause.

The next ten minutes were filled with football talk, Ricky Ellson not always sure of his facts, but being corrected politely by Branruff. Peter Normande asked a couple of pertinent questions, which Branruff also answered.

Bob Grayling was on one knee beside Camera Two counting off on his fingers, "six, five, four . . . . "

"We have to pause for these messages," Ricky said. "But we'll be right back."

In the control room the audio was shut off, but the monitors from the three cameras showed the panel talking together in pantomime. Mina Parelli leaned towards the football star until she was almost in his lap, her pulled-up dress showing an expanse of skinny right thigh.

Peterson opened his mike and told Bob Grayling, "Tell that Parelli dame, for the final time, to pull her dress down or I'll shoot the rest of the show around her. Make sure she understands it's instructions, or orders, from me."

"Right, Norm," Bob Grayling said.

Peterson, the switcher and the script girl watched Grayling passing on Peterson's orders to the Parelli woman. She tossed her head and reluctantly pulled her dress down an inch. Grayling appeared on camera again, speaking to her with some finality. She stood up, let her dress fall to her knees, and seemed to say something sarcastic to Grayling as he walked off camera.

Bellingham Turner spoke across the others in the panel to Jeremy Cronitz. "Bellamy is my Christian name. My family name is Turner."

Peter Normande said to Cronitz laughingly, "And don't you forget it, Cronitz."

Cronitz answered, "Is impossible for man to call himself *Christian* artist." He was scowling now at Turner.

On the stage monitor the mimed commercials went on. A housewife in tears because she'd run out of her favorite detergent; a muffler shop, part of a country-wide chain, containing more cars and their drivers than anyone had ever seen in any of their shops in their lives; a movie feature player, who'd done his last acting years before, selling "Sunland" airplane charter flights; a network promo pushing a late night movie to be aired later that evening; and finally a food chain that insisted its prices were lower than those of any other store in Canada.

Ricky Ellson, who had been talking shop with Peter Normande, looked at Bob Grayling who was mouthing his countdown.

"Ready, everybody," Ricky warned.

The red light flashed on Camera Two and Ricky returned to where he'd left off. To Branruff, "Jim, you're a graduate of South Carolina State, I understand. What happened to your Southern accent?"

Branruff gave a short laugh. "I never acquired one, Rick. I'm a Pennsylvania boy by birth. As it happened I was offered a football scholarship by S.C.S. and went there when I came home from the Nam."

"Vietnam?"

"Yes."

"Where did you serve there?"

"Oh, a lot of places I'd just as soon forget the names of, Rick."

"Were you in the army?"

Branruff was embarrassed by the questioning. His wide white smile had been replaced by a slight frown. "No. U.S. Marine Corps."

Peterson said to the floor director, "Tell Ellson to get off that military shit, Bob."

"Were you an enlisted man?" Ellson asked, showing the viewing audience that he was familiar with American military terms.

"No, I was an officer," Branruff said, his anger showing.

110

Bob Grayling symbolically cut his throat when he caught Ellson's eye and illustrated a change back to football questions with signals that symbolized the carrying and throwing of a football.

"Were you satisfied with your education at South Carolina, Jim?" asked Ellson.

The smile returned to Branruff's face. "Yes, it was a good school. I didn't go there just to play football."

"I've been told that most football scholarships allow their recipients to skip courses and more or less goof around as campus jocks."

Branruff's face was hardening into a warning mask.

"Did you graduate, Jim?" asked the moderator, either not paying attention to Branruff's change of mood or trying to impress both his audience and Peter Normande that he was a thorough investigative reporter.

Branruff answered, his face blank and his eyes boring into Ellson's, "I graduated *summa cum laude* in philosophy."

Peter Normande stepped into the breach. "Jim also has a Phi Beta Kappa key, Ricky."

Peterson flicked his switch and said to Bob Grayling in the studio, "Thank God we've got Peter Normande on the show. Get that stupid son of a bitch Ellson back onto football before Branruff tosses him into the audience. And tell him to stay on the subject!"

"Will do, Norm."

Grayling caught Ellson's attention and frantically mimed football actions, silently mouthing the word "football."

Bellingham Turner was now staring at the black man in the next chair with something like awed respect.

Ellson said, "I guess that's enough about your background, Jim. We'll go back to football."

Branruff stared at him but said nothing. Neither did he smile.

"How do you compare our Canadian game with U.S. football?"

"The field is wider, which gives me more running room," Branruff answered, unsmiling.

For the rest of the football player's question-and-answer period, the questioning being done by Ellson and Normande, the others in the panel were silent. Mina Parelli stared into the black man's face with unashamed lust, Bellingham Turner had returned to his literary hauteur, and only Jeremy Cronitz had the stupidity to break in. He said, "Not to me can a silly game be compared to artistic distinction." His words didn't go out on the network, but one of the cameras focussed on him momentarily.

Peterson said over his mike, "Camera One, stay off Cronitz. Get back to Branruff."

By this time Branruff was smilingly answering Peter Normande's technical questions, and Ricky Ellson was being ignored, off camera.

Norman Peterson leaned back in his chair at the control panel and said, "Whew!" He took out a Kleenex and wiped the sweat from his forehead. He spoke to Bob Grayling. "Tell Ellson to switch to the Parelli woman."

Grayling, standing beside Camera Two, pointed at Mina Parelli.

Ricky Ellson came to life and said, "And now let me introduce the beautiful distaff side of tonight's panel guests." His voice rising. "A lady distinguished as one of this city's best-known hostesses and social-ites, wife, mother, social activist . . . . " Throws up his hands. "I could go on and on, but let me introduce – Ms Mina Parelli!"

There was a scattering of grudging applause as Mina fixed her face in what she hoped was a patrician smile.

Ellson went on. "Tonight Ms Parelli is going to demonstrate a new addition to milady's wardrobe, some of her fabulous headwear which she calls the Parelli Headkerchief."

Scattered handclapping.

"First though, Mina – may I call you that?"

She pursed her lips and gave him a gracious, modest smile.

"Terrific!" Ricky enthused, as if Queen Elizabeth had told him he could call her "Liz." "You've had a fabulous career, I understand. Making you way up to the position you hold today from beginnings that were – humble, to say the least."

In a high-pitched voice that was also harsh rather than husky Mina said, "My family was middle class. For a short time after my father passed away I suppose we could have been called genteely poor."

Peterson murmured, "Christ, one of those!"

Sylvia, the script girl, smiled into her stopwatch.

Before Ellson could begin his obsequious introduction again, Peter Normande chimed in, "Down in our old neighborhood, Mina, we were all working class poor."

Norm Peterson flipped his voice switch and said, "Camera Three pick up Normande and hold on him." He turned to Alex, the switcher, but that unflappable young man already had Three's picture of Normande on its monitor.

Mina said, patrician smile again, "I'm sorry to hear that, Mr. Normande."

Normande laughed. "You don't get it, Mina. *My* old neighborhood was both mine and *yours.* You lived on Wolseley Street near Bathurst and Queen, and I lived on Phoebe, off Spadina."

She was shocked into momentary silence, but then she said, "I think you're making a mistake." She glared at him.

"No I'm not. We went to the same school. Ryerson Public School, on Grange Avenue. We didn't know each other then, you were a grade ahead of me, but I've always remembered you." With a conciliatory smile, "Come on, Mina, confess. It's nothing to be ashamed of. Plenty of successful people have come out of that neighborhood."

Turning away from Normande Mina said to Ricky Ellson, her voice now quavering and her face softened by its desperate plea, "Shall I demonstrate my Headkerchiefs now?"

Ellson answered, "Sure, Mina. Can you take off your mike?"

With Branruff's help she unclasped the neck microphone and stood up.

Peterson said to Bob Grayling on the floor, "Take Camera Three off Normande. Cue Parelli to stage right, have Three follow her, and cue the boom man."

"Roger, Norm."

Peterson again. "Bob, cue Ellson to begin his patter about the handker — Headkerchiefs. In the meantime we'll stay on Two with Rick."

"Okay."

Cronitz said to his dead microphone, off camera and audio, "Grange is where art gallery is. Petit bourgeois institution, not recognize true artist."

Some young people in the front seats guffawed as they heard the old man's remark.

"What the hell is the laughter about?" Peterson asked.

Alex said, "His mike's still cut off."

Sylvia answered, "I think it was something old Cronitz said."

Peterson said to Bob Grayling, "Get Ellson into the act. Tell him to quit dragging his ass."

Ricky Ellson faced Camera Two and began, reading from a cue card held up by a young man standing to the left of the camera. "Now, for the ladies in the viewing audience, and for the men too who will purchase them for their wives and sweethearts, Ms Mina Parelli will now demonstrate the newest thing in feminine headwear, the Headkerchief." He half turned in his chair and swept his arm to where Mina was standing in the light from a junior spot, under the mike boom. Beside her stood a small table holding a collection of vari-colored Headkerchiefs.

In her high harsh voice the Parelli woman began her spiel, reading amateurishly from a second cue card substituted by the young man standing beside Camera Two. He was at least a yard to the left of the camera, so that on the control booth monitors, and also on every TV set tuned into the program, it was apparent that instead of a faked spontaneity by the speaker talking into the camera eye Mina was reading her lines as she stared somewhere to the camera's left.

Peterson flipped his mike switch and said, "Bob, get that kid with the cue cards right up against Number Two."

Grayling moved the cue-card boy over against the camera.

"The Headkerchief was designed by me for casual wear," Mina said. "It can be worn as a head covering during a shower – a rain shower that is – " No laughter, not even a titter from the audience. "It can be worn as a hair-protector at the beach, in a car, anywhere the modern woman wishes to keep her coiffured hair in place, and protected."

She picked one up from the table and held it lightly with a finger. "Made up in a variety of gay with-it colors and patterns, of light foulard silk, it fits easily into purse, pocket or your car's glove compartment. It can also be worn in a variety of styles, and fastens with a patented elastic frill." Picking up first one then another of the pieces from the table she demonstrated the various ways each could be worn and fastened on the head with a pair of tapered tails.

"What do you think of them, Sylvia?" Peterson asked.

"I think they're great. The only thing is they're not Mrs. Parelli's

creation at all. They're been demonstrated already in the department stores."

"Then what's she doing flogging them on this show?"

"I guess she's been hired to demonstrate them."

"Who put her on?" Peterson asked the girl angrily.

"I guess I and Rick did, Norm. We had a phone call yesterday from Mr. Collisher asking us to. Telling us to, really."

Peterson rubbed his hair over his eyes and stared tight-lipped at the monitors.

Sylvia began her countdown to the final commercials.

Automatically Norm Peterson cued Bob Grayling on the floor. "Bob, when we go into the commercials fade out Parelli, have the boom man move off, and bring Camera Two back to Rick. Remember we have two minutes before the credits. As soon as you hear the theme music pull the two cameras that aren't shooting the credits back to a slow fade-out, then have one of them pan across the studio audience for the final applause."

"Gotcha, Norm."

Peterson said to himself, "What the hell is that son of a bitch Collisher trying to do? Network general manager my ass! An old school chum of McLaughlin's that's all. Without McLaughlin he couldn't get a job plucking chickens!"

Sylvia ended her countdown and the first commercial came on the control room monitor.

The telephone at Sylvia's elbow rang, and she answered it. Turning to Peterson, her hand covering the mouthpiece she said, "It's Mr. Collisher, Norm."

"Tell him I'll talk to him after the show. Not now."

Sylvia repeated the message into the phone.

Over the muted audio from the commercials Peterson could hear Collisher screaming at the other end of the telephone line. Sylvia held the phone in her hand.

"Okay, kid, give it to me," Peterson said, taking the phone from the girl. "Listen, Collisher, you bullying bastard, I've got a show on the tube, and I can't talk to you right now. What the hell's the idea of putting that skinny mistress of yours on to flog those goddam headbands of hers. Maybe Mr. McLaughlin would like to hear how you give

away commercial time on his network. Anyhow, by the looks of things from here, that acey-deucey Parelli broad has found a new temporary lover, Jim Branruff." He slammed the phone into its cradle.

Flipping his floor mike switch he said quietly to Bob Grayling, "Bob, cue Ellson to go into his final give-and-take with Normande and Turner, maybe Branruff. Stay off the Parelli woman and old Cronitz."

"Okay, Norm."

After the end of commercial countdown Ricky Ellson said, "We only have enough time for a few give-and-takes with our guests." He turned to Bellingham Turner and asked, "Are you working on a new book, Mr. Turner?"

The author's face came alive with its public haughtiness and he answered, "I'm afraid my literary endeavors are in a state of fallow at present."

Ricky, who had been expecting more, turned quickly to Jim Branruff. "I suppose you'll be returning home, Jim, until football training begins?"

"Yes, Rick, I'll be back then."

"All your fans will be looking forward to seeing you next summer."

"Thank you."

Despite Grayling's frantic hand-waving, Mina Parelli crossed the stage between the cameras and the panel and sat down in her chair, searching behind her for her microphone.

In the control room Peterson sat back in his chair and laughed. "I don't believe it!" he said through his laughter. "I never believed it could happen, but it has!"

Ellson asked Peter Normande, "Was this show more hectic than your radio hot line, Peter?"

"A little *more* frantic, I'd say."

Bellingham Turner, off camera, said, "That's the first apt comment you've made tonight, Normande."

Normande turned in his chair and said, "Yes. It's too bad really, Turner, Bellingham, or whatever your real unliterary name is. For instance I wanted to ask you why *you* came back to Canada from Oxford or wherever during the Second World War while the real Canadian men were going *to* England to fight?"

Turner answered, leering in the radio performer's direction, "I don't

116

have to answer a slum neighborhood upstart's reflections on my patriotism. Perhaps you should ask your own immigrant father what *he* did during the war."

Peterson said to Bob Grayling, "Keep a camera on Turner and one on Normande."

"What about the credits, Norm?"

"Fuck the credits." To Sylvia he said, "Excuse me, baby."

Down in the studio Ricky Ellson was motioning excitedly to Grayling, who was paying him no attention. Instead he was staring openmouthed at Turner and Normande.

Normande unhooked his microphone and holding it before his face said, *"My* father, you useless parasite, is in a war cemetery in Holland. In a grave with a Star of David on it − "

Turner gave a disinterested shrug.

"And with his real name, Private Abraham Norlovsky on it."

Turner gave a sneering smile and said, "I'm glad to hear *some* of your kind went to war."

Normande dropped his microphone, ran across the front of the panel, and planted a hard right in Turner's face. Turner's chair tipped over backwards.

Peterson said into the floor mike, "Bob, stay with the action."

As Normande's camera followed him the viewing audience caught a glimpse of Jeremy Cronitz leaning forward in his chair, the laughing face of Jim Branruff, and of Mina Parelli clutching the black football player tightly.

Camera Two showed a dazed Bellingham Turner, his bottom lip running blood, scrambling to his feet and unmindful of the chest microphone that held him tethered trying to escape off the set. Peter Normande was climbing over the spilled chair. Ricky Ellson was shouting, "Stop it! Stop it!" over his open microphone.

Bob Grayling shouted into his mike, "Norm what'll I do!"

Peterson answered, "Get a pan shot of the audience, but keep one camera on the fight."

"I can't do that, Norm. For chrissakes we'll all be fired!"

You won't be, Bob, just me. Get the studio audience reaction!"

One of the cameras panned slowly across the audience. Everyone was standing up, some of the women holding their hands over their faces in terror, some men laughing, and almost everyone either shouting or screaming in a mixture of bewilderment, horror or laughter.

The switcher, without being cued by Peterson, put on the theme music, and the cameras slowly faded to black.

"Thanks, Akex," Peterson said, as the switcher flipped down most of his toggles and switches.

When Ricky Ellson tried to contact the control room over the floor director's headset and mike he was told by Sylvia that Norm Peterson had left. He handed the headset back to Grayling and watched the audience filing from the studio, now laughing, talking animatedly to each other, strangers or not, and some slapping each other on the back.

From behind him on the studio speakers came his own voice, taped. His voice said, "Tune in again next week, ladies and gentlemen, for the eight hundred and fifth return of What Gives?"

From the exiting audience a voice shouted, "Or maybe the fourth re-run of *Lassie*."

Normande and Jeremy Cronitz were nowhere to be seen, but the cameramen, grips and gaffers were gathered together in an excited knot in the centre of the stage. Mina Parelli and Jim Branruff were making their exit following the crowd through the street entrance. They were circling each other with their arms.

Across the stage came the tall but no longer dignified figure of Bellingham Turner, a bloody handkerchief pressed to his mouth. "Hey, you," he muttered through his cut and swollen lips.

Ricky Ellson ignored him.

"You! You there! Ellson!"

"What do *you* want?"

"Who's in charge around here?"

"At this time of night hardly anybody. Try the news department." He swung on his heel and made his way towards the stage entrance.

"Ellson!"

Ricky ignored him again.

"Ellson I'm suing you and the station for a lot of money. You've publicly humiliated me!"

Ricky turned then and said, "Listen, you big phony bastard, you humiliated yourself before a million viewers. To say nothing of ruining a show that's been a success for the past four years. The only person you can sue is Peter Normande for punching you in the mouth, something somebody should have done years ago. I wouldn't bother though if I were you, because you're going to get enough flack as it is from the Jewish community. You may even receive a visit from the Jewish Defence League. As for me, if you charge Normande with assault, I'll be *his* witness not yours. Why don't you just toddle back to Rosedale or wherever the hell you live and think things over carefully before tomorrow morning."

He turned again, waved to the now silent group of technicians in the centre of the stage, and made his way through the door.

When he reached the small cubicle of an office that he shared with another talk show host he donned his overcoat. Without bothering to remove his make-up he walked slowly out to the parking lot and got into his car.

THE OLD MAN'S LAUGHTER

There was no doubt about it, they were all waiting for the old man to die. He used to sit in the rocking chair between the wood-box and the kitchen stove, a lonely grizzled old figure as lean and straight as a balsam. He would watch them as they entered the house, waiting for one of them to speak to him, taking his place at the table after the others had eaten. They seldom acknowledged his presence, but their attitude did not seem to fire his anger. Instead, he seemed to be secretly laughing at them — laughing as an eighty-year-old man does behind the burned-up wrinkled skin of his face.

In the evenings when they thought he was asleep they would argue about the division of his, their grandfather's farm and and money; Ella insisting that she should get the house and land by right of possession, and her brothers Wilfred and Roy ready to settle for the thousand dollars they knew he had in the bank.

One of the few times the old man ever roused himself was the day one of his granddaughter Ella's children took his pipe from the arm of his rocking chair and lost it in the weeds behind the house. He shouted then, waving a palsied hand, "Elly, get me my pipe back! It's the only comfort I've got left around here since your Granny died. I know what you're waiting for, but none of you'll benefit from my death — not one of you!"

Ella told him not to act like a silly old fool, and took her own good time finding his pipe. She returned it to him with a look on her mean pinched face that was almost a snarl. She had ignored what he'd said about nobody benefiting when he died; he'd not drawn up a will, didn't have a lawyer, and was unable to write one on his own as he was illiterate.

The only effect of his momentary anger was to unleash again that strong deep voice which reminded them all that he had once been young and virile; a man who had cleared the farm from the surrounding forest. It was said along that part of the Gaspe Coast that in his prime, using an axe and bucksaw, he'd been known to cut and stack four cords of pulpwood a day, and had been the first man to drive a team and portage sleigh from New Carlisle to Quebec. If their eagerness and greed hadn't blinded them to everything else they'd have realized that a man like that doesn't allow himself to be trampled on without a struggle.

There finally came the day when Grandpa took to his bed for the last time. His grandchildren were happy not to find him sitting in the kitchen every time they came in, glancing at them with a look that was formed more of sorrow than contempt. Neither of the brothers ever went upstairs to his room, and the only sign, to them, that he was still alive was the sound of a dry cough now and again, or a feeble call to their sister Ella.

They agreed among themselves that it was a shame they were forced to work in the woods when Grandpa had money in the bank, and one day Wilfred said to Roy, "We could buy that truck off of Joe Simard if we had six hundred dollars."

"Sure we could, only we haven't got six hundred," Roy answered, spitting his cud of tobacco towards the kitchen stove.

"If we had a truck we could haul pulpwood all summer, and the truck would soon pay for itself," his brother went on, brushing a large hand across his stubbled chin.

"Where could we get the money?" Roy asked.

Wilfred raised his eyes and looked at the ceiling below Grandpa's room.

"That old fool would never give it to us," Roy said.

"It wouldn't do no harm to try."

They climbed the stairs to the old man's room and stood together against the foot of the iron bed. Roy edged behind the wider bulk of his brother as Grandpa stared at them from beneath the old army blanket that covered him, his eyes running over their faces as he tried to see into their thoughts. Beside him on the old mirrorless dresser lay his pipe and tobacco pouch and a yellowing photograph of their grandmother.

"It's nice of you to come up to see me, boys," the old man said happily as he pushed himself up with an elbow.

"Grandpa — " Wilfred began.

"Yes, Wilfred?" Grandpa asked, trying to smile through quivering lips.

"We wondered if you could loan us six hundred dollars. We know where we can buy a good truck cheap, and we figured we could haul pulp this summer."

The old man's smile was replaced by a look of sorrow. "I should have known you'd want something, but I hoped you might have dropped up here to see how I was getting along." His voice had lost its timbre over the months, and now it had the sound of death about it.

Roy got angry then and shouted, "What good is it having that money laying there in the bank doing nothing! Why don't you let us have enough to buy a truck!"

"It's not the money," the old man said. He stared at Roy a long time before he shook his head sadly. "I never expected that you'd turn out like the others," he said.

Roy felt a slight wave of shame rising over his neck and ears at the sound of the old man's words. He remembered the times when Grandpa had taken him with him into the woods when he was a small boy, imparting to him all the lore he'd learned through eighty years of living. And of the time, after their parents had died, when Grandpa had scraped together the money to keep him in school. Without another word he turned and left the room. As he descended the stairs he heard Wilfred say, "I don't see why you won't let us have the money now. You'll be dead soon, anyhow, and we'll have it then!"

Then for the first time he heard his grandfather sobbing.

During the next few weeks Grandpa weakened fast, hardly able any more to move around on the bed. One spring evening as the others were sitting in the kitchen they heard him cry out to Ella. She finished washing up the dishes remaining from her husband's supper before going up to Grandpa's room.

When she returned, the others asked what the old man had wanted. She shrugged her skinny shoulders and tapped her forehead. "He asked me to prop him up so he could look out the window. When I did, he looked out at the woods and fields. He said, "I know them hills better'n any man alive.' I asked him what he meant, but all he did was grin, then fell back again into the bed."

"He won't last much longer," Wilfred said, unable to keep his satisfaction to himself.

"The way he looks I don't expect him to live out the week," Ella agreed.

Before the end of the week it seemed nothing remained alive of Grandpa but the dull fire of his eyes staring out from beneath the rumpled old army blanket.

On the following Saturday Ella and her husband drove the children to her sister-in-law's place in Pointe-à-la-Garde. After they were gone the old man called downstairs to his grandsons, and they went up to his room.

"Is Ella gone?" the old man asked.

Roy nodded.

"I don't think I'll live out the night," he said.

Neither of the boys answered him.

"I want you two to go to town and bring back the priest."

They stood in indecision at the foot of the bed, Wilfred wearing a half-smirk on his face, his hands inside the bib of his overalls. Roy scuffed his feet on the floorboards while his eyes shifted to the dirty glass of the window.

"Surely you can do this much for me," Grandpa begged. "It'll be the last thing I'll ever ask you to do."

Roy looked at his brother and said, "We might as well."

Without asking the old man if they could do anything else for him, the two of them went downstairs and left the house.

It was late evening when they returned with the priest in tow. The house was in darkness, and Roy lighted a lamp and led the priest up the stairs to Grandpa's room.

The bed was standing stark and empty against the wall, the army blanket tossed in a trailing pile at its foot. Grandpa's old clothes were missing from their nail above the bed, but his ancient Sunday suit – his burial clothes – was still hanging in its accustomed place. On the top of the broken dresser lay his pipe and tobacco. The photograph of their Grandma was gone.

"He won't have gone very far without his pipe," Roy said in surprise. He shouted to Wilfred, and together with the puzzled priest they searched the house and yard for the old man, without success. When Ella and her family returned the next day they gathered a few of the neighbors together and searched the woods bordering on the fields behind the house.

"It's just like him to run away now and put us to the job of looking for him," Ella said. "He always had a contrary streak."

"What's the difference whether *we* have to bury him or he buries himself in the woods somewheres?" Wilfred asked. "It saves us the funeral money anyways."

His sister and brother agreed with him, and during the next few days they contented themselves with a few token searches of the woods roundabout, more for appearance's sake than anything else.

At the end of the first week they notified the Provincial Police about the old man's disappearance, and a senior officer and some uniformed men with a tracking dog arrived at the house. The officer told them that due to the rain that had fallen, and the length of time it had taken the family to notify the Q.P.P. in Matapedia, it would be almost impossible now to pick up the old man's trail; at least the dog couldn't do it.

Without Grandpa around, Ella began lording it over her brothers, reminding them that the house was now hers, making them wash nearly every day and even scrape their feet when they came in from the barn. Just like everyone else they were puzzled how a sloppy housekeeper like Ella had suddenly become so finicky about some things.

After what they figured was a decent two-week interval the brothers went down to the bank in town to claim the estate. "We've come for the money our grandfather left us," Wilfred said to the bank manager, sitting down, uninvited, on a chair and pushing his hat to the back of his head.

"The money your grandfather left you?" asked the manager. "Is he dead?"

"Of course he's dead!" Wilfred snarled. Then with a short laugh he said, "If he didn't die the night he sneaked off into the woods, he's sure as Christ dead by now!"

The bank manager tried to hide his disgust as he asked, "You have no proof of his death, have you?"

"We don't need proof. Everybody knows he was on his death bed. Nobody as old and sick as he was could have lived this long alone in the woods," Wilfred answered, getting mad.

"You'll need definite proof," the manager explained, trying to hold his temper. "Without finding his body or other definite proof that your grandfather is no longer alive you'll have to wait a long, long time before anything can be done."

Wilfred began to rave and curse, so the bank manager had them thrown into the street.

125

When they reached home and told their sister what the bank manager had said, she laughed. "I knew I was the smartest one. I've still got the house and land anyways. And you two might as well know right now that me and my family needs it for ourselves. So you can both get out!"

A week later a storekeeper in St. Omer, an old friend of Grandpa's, foreclosed an unknown mortgage on the farm, and Ella and her family were forced to leave the place too.

During the fall Ella and her family moved to Ontario, but her brothers stayed in the district, searching the woods for their grandfather's body. The strain became too much for Wilfred, who had roamed the forest, streams and roads around the neighborhood, unshaven and with a wild crazy look in his eye, scaring everyone he met. He would tell eyeryone who couldn't escape meeting him that he could hear the old man's laughter everywhere he went. In the spring they took him away to the mental hospital in Rimouski, and Roy disappeared shortly afterwards.

The old man's body still lies hidden somewhere in the woods. The superstitious people around these parts have reported hearing the dry cackle of his laugh as they went about their work or travelled back and forth to town.

Of course I *don't believe that! When I hear the old man's laughter I pretend that it's only the noise of the wind through the fir and spruce trees.*

A WALK ON Y STREET

It certainly looked like Tom Lengers strolling down the street ahead of him, but he couldn't be sure. After an interval of years even the way a person walks is changed, and on a street as crowded as Y Street is on a fine Saturday afternoon, a stranger can take on the appearance of a long-remembered friend out of the past.

Not that he'd consciously been looking for Tommy, but on occasion he'd had warm memories of his boyhood friend, and knew he was here in the city somewhere. Once, not long after he'd married but before they'd moved out to Maple Heights, he'd pointed out Tom's name to Gloria when he'd spotted it in a TV drama's closing credits. "Sets by Thomas Lengers," it had said. He'd bragged to his bride about knowing Tommy since they were children, and had been happy to discover his old friend was doing so well.

Back in Curranville Tommy Lengers had been the son of the local druggist, and they'd gone through elementary school together. Later he himself had gone on to the high school in a nearby larger town, while Tommy had come to the city to study art, first at a technical school and later at art college. Tommy had always been at the top of the class in his art work, and used to design the costumes and sets for the Christmas and Easter pageants. Even Mrs. Emily Carson Roberts, Curranville's historian and chairlady of the Pen Club, whose district history was in the Smathers Bay public library, had once said, "Tommy has a wild but genuine artistic talent."

He began walking much faster than he usually did on his Saturday afternoon strolls, trying to catch up with the man ahead. It was hard to reduce the distance between them very fast due to the crowds on the sidewalk.

The Saturday strollers on Y Street had changed greatly over the past few years. Once they had been people like himself, walking downtown to shop or take in an early dinner or a movie, now there were many Blacks, the odd Indian or Pakistani wearing a turban or sari, and a statistical majority of sloppily dressed members of the younger generation with uncut hair and wildly anarcho-hobo clothes. These young people were slightly distasteful to him, though he sometimes secretly envied their flaunting of their individuality.

As he closed the gap between himself and the figure he was following he remembered his last conversation with Tommy. It had happened on his final visit to Curranville, before his parents had left the town and moved permanently to Florida. Though he was married to Gloria at the time he was still only an assistant accountant with the Stock Exchange branch of the bank. Gloria still had her teaching job, and they were spending every penny they made on their new house.

Tommy had also been visiting Curranville that weekend, and was helping out in his father's drugstore. He had sensed a change in Tommy the moment they'd exchanged pleasantries, an artiness he supposed he could call it. They had talked briefly across the drugstore counter, Tommy mentioning that he was interested in "getting into merchandising from a design point of view," or something which sounded like that. He had been a little surprised at the new way Tommy seemed to talk.

Before leaving the drugstore he told Tommy about his marriage and their new house in Maple Heights, and had invited his friend to visit them soon. He distinctly recalled Tommy jotting down his phone number. "Gloria and I would love to have you and your girl friend up to the house for dinner and a drink," he'd said. Neither young Carol nor Spence had been born then, so it must have been ten years ago at least.

There had been no phone call from Tommy, and he knew it was not because Maple Heights had been a twenty-five cent toll call in those days. He'd guessed that his old friend had his own circle of acquaintances by now, designers and people like that, and he and Gloria were not what could be called artistic types. As a matter of fact he supposed they would be looked down upon as dull squares by Tom and his friends, who were part of the art world you might say.

He dodged back and forth from the edge of the sidewalk to the store fronts, giving the hippies and wierdos a wide berth while still keeping the figure up ahead in view. He'd got into the habit of driving downtown on Saturday afternoons, parking his car in a lot north of the business section and walking down Y Street the mile and a half or so to the department stores before retracing his route to the parking lot. Excepting his weekday lunch-hour walks through the financial district and nine holes of Sunday golf in the summer it was the only exercise he took.

Today was one of those early spring afternoons when it was warm enough to discard gloves and scarf but still cool enough to wear a topcoat. Some male walkers were not wearing coats at all, but since he'd had his mild coronary he'd faithfully followed his doctor's advice, not babying himself by any means but not being careless either.

Len Adams was their family doctor, and they both belonged to the Kinsmen and the Maple Heights Golf & Country Club. Len had been a regular golf partner of his for years, but since government health insurance Len hadn't had as much time as he'd had formerly to play. The course wasn't what it had once been either, and this he blamed on the calibre of the new citizens of the Heights, who were – well, more common than the original home-owners.

He skipped past a pair of long-haired freaks wearing camouflaged ponchos or whatever they called them, and fell into step behind the man he was now certain was Tom Lengers. His quarry was fairly tall, and though his hair was longer than they would stand for down at the bank, it was short in contrast to the long dirty mops of some of the others on the street. He also walked in the careless round-shouldered way his friend had walked. By the time he reached the man's side he was positive it was Tom, despite the dark glasses he wore.

The man suddenly stopped and stared into an art store window. He stopped too, as if he was also interested in the single painting on display. He glanced surreptitiously at the man's face; it was Tommy Lengers all right, the small scar running up from one corner of his mouth being all the identification he needed.

The other stared at the painting as if entranced, but to him it was just a decorative arrangement of stripes and blocks of heavy paint, not the sort of thing he or his neighbors would want to hang above their fireplace.

Despite his lack of breath after hurrying to catch up with the other he whispered, "Hi, Tommy."

The man turned his head and appeared to look down on him, though the dark glasses hid his eyes. His pressed lips showed no sign of recognition. "Hello," he said.

"Bill Bretford, Tommy – from Curranville."

"Sure." The other's face lighted up. "Willie!" He offered his hand.

It had been years since anyone had called him Willie.

"I felt sure it was you," Bill told him. "I've been trying to catch up to you for more than a block."

"This street's fairly crowded on Saturdays," Tommy said still holding Bill's hand. Bill noticed once again how his friend's voice had changed, perhaps not his voice exactly but the way he pronounced his words. They were sort of precise and – well, put on. Not at all like the way he remembered Tommy talking as a boy. Bill guessed it was the way artistic people learned to talk.

"I wasn't sure it was you at first," Bill said. "It was only when I got close enough to notice the way you walked – "

"Walked!" Tommy dropped his hand.

"Yeah. You know, sort of stoop-shouldered, the way I remembered you. Then the scar on your lip clinched it."

"Oh," Tommy said, smiling again.

"A minute ago, when you were looking at that painting, I said to myself, 'That's Tommy Lengers all right.'"

The taller man was still smiling but he turned his face away from the other as he said, "The day I got that scar was a long time ago, Willie."

"It sure was. My goodness it must have been thirty years ago!"

"Not quite that long, Willie." As if to change the subject he asked, "What are you doing these days?"

"I'm still with the bank," Bill told him. "Head office now. Foreign Exchange."

"Groovy! Let's see, you married a girl from Craig Siding, didn't you?"

"No," Bill said, a little hurt that his friend had forgotten. "You must be thinking of Charley Summers. I married Gloria when I first came down to the city. She was a probationary nurse then."

"That Charley Summers!" Tommy removed his – shades, as Bill's son called them, tilted his head back and closed his eyes, impervious to anything else Bill had said. "He had shoulders like Buster Crabbe." Opening his eyes and smiling to himself as if to a secret memory he asked, "Remember the old Tarzan serial at the movie house in Smathers Bay?"

"The Huron Theatre," Bill provided, laughing.

"I used to imagine Charley as Tarzan." Recovering with a small start and putting on his galsses again. "How is – Gloria, Willie?"

"Fine, Tommy. Of course she had a little woman trouble last winter, but Len Adams, he's our family G.P., said most women her age can

130

expect that sort of thing. She's feeling pretty good ag – "

"I'm sorry I forgot your wife's name for a minute," Tom said.

"That's all right." He couldn't be sure but he thought he'd noticed Lengers wince when he'd mentioned Len Adams, or maybe it had been Gloria's illness. A chasm had suddenly opened up between them, as if they now inhabited different worlds where wives and first-name family doctors were the subjects of conversation on one side but taboo on the other. Or maybe Tom's crowd didn't refer to their wives by their first names to those who'd never met them.

In Maple Heights all the husbands referred to their wives by name; it was the social thing to do, at least by those individual home-owners who'd opened up the suburb. Some of the apartment-dwellers who now lived there called them "my wife," or even "*the* wife," which had always struck him as, well, a little vulgar and working class.

"I guess your children are really coming along?" Tom asked, in an uninterested way, bringing his eyes back to Bill's from something or someone he'd been staring at over the shorter man's shoulder. He put on his glasses again, being careful not to disturb the hair over his ears.

"Yes. Carol was married last June, and Spence is attending military college."

"Groovy, Willie." Tom threw up his hands and dropped his fingers limply in an involuntary gesture. "Let's not talk about such things; they make us seem so *terribly* old." He laughed without laughing at all, as Bill had noticed some of the juniors do at directional-activation meetings at the bank.

Bill had already noticed that Tom was dressed pretty young-looking for a man his age, and "groovy" was a word that belonged to his son Spence's generation. Though it was still chilly Tom wore no topcoat over his green double-breasted suit, yellow shirt and wide brown necktie. Bill glanced down at the other's shoes, which were light brown snakeskin loafers. It was Tom's hair though that puzzled him. It was not greying as his was over the ears, but had a waved grey streak running back from his forehead. Bill was sure Tom's hair had been dyed that way, or "styled" as they now called it. It was a million miles away from the two-bit haircuts they used to get at Jonesy's barber shop in Curran-ville, and at least a thousand miles from the shopping plaza barbering in Maple Heights.

131

"I used to see your name on TV play credits," Bill said to break the silence. "That was quite a while ago. You used to design the sets, didn't you?"

"Something like that," the other answered. He didn't seem too happy that Bill had brought the subject up.

"What do you do now, Tom?"

The tall man was pretending to look at the painting again, but Bill had the feeling he was staring at his reflection in the window.

"What?" he asked, turning quickly as if caught in an embarrassing act. "Oh. Oh, I'm supervising the display department down at Gregory's," he said, naming one of the city's minor department stores. "Advisory mostly."

"A window dresser?"

For some reason this seemed to anger him and he answered sharply, "Of course not, silly."

Bill, taken aback by the other's quick flash of anger, said hurriedly, "I'm glad you got into the line of work you wanted to. That time I talked to you in your father's drugstore, remember? You told me then you wanted to go into display design."

With pursed lips the other man stared at him. When he relaxed his lips he said, "My gawd, Willie, you haven't forgotten anything, have you?"

"Not much," Bill answered, smiling. "Is the drugstore still in Curranville?"

"Yes, but the old man sold out to a drug chain years ago."

"Old man?" One thing he hadn't forgotten was that Tom had always called Mr. Lengers "Father," not Dad or Pop or whatever the other kids had called their male parent. He didn't mention this but asked, "How *are* your mother and father, Tom?"

'Both gone. A long time now."

It surprised him that Tom could be so offhand about his parents passing away. He remembered Mrs. Lengers as a very nice lady who used to give him and Tom slices of buttered bread spread with brown sugar after school.

Tom had turned his head and seemed to be watching two young men who passed behind them on the sidewalk, though it was really hard to be sure what he was staring at from behind his shades. When

132

they had disappeared in the crowd Tom turned and said, "It's been *so* good seeing you again, Willie. We'll have to get together soon and have lunch or something."

"I forgot, Tom, to ask if you're married. Perhaps you and your wife or lady friend would like to come out to our home for dinner with Gloria and me?"

A corner of Lenger's lips turned up in a cut-off smile as he said, "Sure, Willie. Love to."

Bill laughed. "We're going in the same direction, Tommy, why don't we walk down the street together?"

As if he'd searched for an excuse but had been unable to find any, Tom said, "Oh, all right."

They walked almost a block without speaking. Bill was wondering if his aroused suspicions about his old friend were correct. He searched back in his memory for some previous indication or behavior on Lengers' part that would substantiate these new-found suspicions.

There had been the Maniwotok County Sports Day held in Smathers Bay one year, the final year that both he and Lengers had spent in Curranville. He remembered sitting in the infield of the old Smathers Bay lacrosse stadium watching the Curranville High Junior Relay Team, of which Lengers was the anchorman, beat both the Duffield and Stowberg teams for the first time in years. After the race he had got up from the grass, wearing his old grey sweatshirt and slacks instead of a sweatsuit (his own event, the mile run, in which he'd been lapped, had finished long before), and joining the other kids in a victory dance in midfield.

During the girls' hurdles and the jumping events he had made his way across the back of the field to the shabby tumbledown dressing rooms under the short rise of bleachers which the visiting teams were using. Mr. McClough, the Curranville High maths teacher who was guarding their team's street clothes, was standing on the back track watching the high jump.

"Too bad, Bretford," he'd said to Bill as he passed.

"Yes, sir."

The dressing room shared by the Curranville and Duffield teams was empty, for both high schools had strong teams in the fifty yard hurdles. However, from behind the closed door of the cold-water shower room Bill heard a boyish giggle followed by the sounds of a struggle and a string of schoolboy curses. As he was removing his sweat-shirt and running shorts the door to the showers opened and Tom Lengers staggered out, holding a towel to his mouth.

Lengers had not answered Bill's question, but had busied himself pulling on his clothes with one hand while holding the towel to his face. Bill had noticed that the other had not even dried himself. Later, after Lengers had left the dressing room, Bill had entered the showers. He found Charley Summers leaning with his back against the smooth wooden walls of one of the three shower stalls, shivering in the cold spray from the shower.

"What happened to Lengers?" Bill asked him.

"What!"

Louder so his voice could be heard over the noise of the shower, Bill asked him again.

Charley shrugged.

"For chrissakes his mouth was cut or something!" Bill shouted.

Charley said something about Lengers fooling around. He didn't elaborate, and Bill entered one of the other stalls.

Though he didn't dawdle too long under the cold shower, by the time he returned to the dressing room Charley had gone.

The evasiveness of both boys had put a wild thought into his head, but he just couldn't believe his friend was that way. He knew about such things of course, but the only person who was even under suspicion of something as remote as that was old man Griswold who owned a men's clothing store in Curranville. There were stories among the high school boys that it was possible to get a pair of slacks for less than the retail price by letting Grissy play with you while he was pretending to take your inside leg measurement.

As far as he knew, Charley Summers had never mentioned the incident with Tommy to anyone else, and over the years it had become blurred and distorted by time in Bill's mind, so that he'd finally accepted the consensus that Tommy's cut lip had happened in a schoolboy fight with Charley Summers over a girl named Loretta Carboy. Now, as they strolled down Y Street his earlier suspicions took over and were corroborated by these new ones.

They passed some young street people selling beads, leather belts and handbags, and a thin frizzy-haired girl sat on the stone steps of a new government office block surrounded by multi-striped homemade heavy candles.

"These hippies are certainly taking over Y Street," Bill said.

"They aren't hippies any more, just kids doing their own thing," Lengers said, staring straight ahead.

Bill felt he'd said something wrong. To cover up his remark, or maybe just to show Lengers he wasn't a square or a snob, he said, "We have them up in Maple Heights too. They — well the young kids are a lot different than we used to be."

There was no answer from Lengers.

They passed a curbside single file of shaven-headed saffron-robed Hare Krishna people, two of them begging or selling their literature to passers-by, the others beating on a small bongo drum, a tiny cymbal, and shaking a string of little bells. They were all chanting. Some wore white-painted stripes on their noses, and one of the young women in the group was carrying a baby in a contraption slung on her back. Bill was afraid to mention them to Lengers after the reception his remark about the hippies had received.

"Tomorrow's our local golf tournament," he said, when they found themselves alone on an empty stretch of sidewalk. "The Kinsmen are sponsoring it. There's a couple of tournament golfers coming up from the States. Do you ever play, Tommy?"

Without looking at him the other shook his head.

"I'm pretty much of a duffer myself," Bill admitted. "Even after ten years at it. I'm looking forward though to getting out there to the club and swinging at a few."

Lengers gave his head a slight turn, and seemed to be examining him condescendingly.

They passed boutiques, health food stores, some two-star restaurants, pornographic book shops, unisex clothing stores, body rub parlors and small blue movie houses "Sit in your own booth; watch your own screen," a crowd of wierdos clustered in front of ROY THE RECORD ROBBER's place of business, army-navy stores whose windows were filled with rifles, binoculars, packsacks, cotton blankets, old World War Two gas-mask bags, stores that sold only imitation leather goods, a joint with old evening gowns and silver slippers that pandered to transvestites, discount electronic outlets, a Hindu restaurant with credit card signs in its window, paperback book shops "Please don't remove the plastic wrapper on this book!", a time-payment furniture store, stores that rented out evening clothes, poster and T-shirt emporiums . . . .

"Hi, Larry."

"Hi." Lengers looked over his shoulder, and Bill followed his example. A blondined young man in a short leather coat was being swallowed up by the crowd behind them.

"Did he call you Larry?" Bill asked.

"Yes. I changed my first name, for professional .rposes, a couple of years back," Lengers answered. "Tommy was — well, too much. I'm now known as Lawrence."

Bill said, "I guess that's what surprised you? Me calling you Tommy when I came up to you in front of the art store?"

"Yes, I haven't been called that for a long time."

They crossed a main east-west street on the green light.

Two obvious homosexuals approached them head on, both staggering a little.

"Larry, dear!" one of them exclaimed as they blocked Bill and his friend. Both gave Bill put-on coquettish smiles.

"Hi, Ross . . . Gerald," Lengers said.

"Who's your new boy friend, Larry?" the short plump one asked.

Lengers went through the introductions hurriedly. Bill got the impression that the taller one of the pair, the one called Gerald, worked with Lengers.

"Where are you two heading?" Lengers asked them.

"Nowhere in particular, dear," Ross answered, staring at Bill as though he were challenging the older man.

"Just a Saturday cruise," said his partner, tittering.

"Where've you just come from?"

"Down at The Livery Stable," Gerald said.

"Anybody there?"

"*Everybody*, darling!" Ross exclaimed, taking his eyes off Bill as if such a suburban square was trespassing on a street now taken over by fags, Jesus freaks and idiots of every color, persuasion and perversion outside the norm on certain days of the week and certain hours of the day.

"Even that goddam closet queen Penfield is there," his friend Gerald put in. "He's surrounded by his — " a quick look at Bill that made him change a word — "entourage. And still putting on the hardhat bit." He pivoted and tried to change his expression to one stern and masculine.

Lengers smiled wanly, but Bill laughed out loud at the chubby man's pantomime.

"Do they serve jug beer at the Stable?" Lengers asked. "I haven't been there since Paul and I broke up, and it was run by the former owners."

"They sell anything you want, honey, except tricks; those you have to find for yourself. Draft by the glass, stein or jug. And get this, Larry, sherry for the old folks. Isn't that a gas! That red-headed bitch Bedard is sitting there with his friend Luke, looking like a pair of Seaton St. landladies sipping their catawba."

Bill realized that the place they were talking about was a renovated pub about a block farther down Y Street that had long been taken over by homosexuals. He was discomfited and repulsed by the returned stare of the one called Ross, who when he caught Bill's eye raised his shaped eyebrows and tossed head back with a provocative smile. Bill quickly turned and glanced at a display of yellowing cough-syrup boxes in the window of a rundown drugstore before which they were standing.

Lengers said something Bill didn't catch, and the others giggled.

"Do you think I'm stoned, Lawrence?" Gerald asked.

Lengers must have confirmed or denied it with a shake or nod of his head, for Bill didn't hear him speak. He remained staring into the store window, wondering how to explain things if someone he knew from Maple Heights or the bank saw him with Lengers and his friends. He turned from the window, his mind made up to leave. He was just in time to catch Lengers, his head tilted towards him, making a square with the thumbs and forefingers of both hands.

"We've got to go, Larry," Gerald said.

"Yes. So-long, sweetie," the short fat one said. Then to his companion, "Let's make the green light, Gerry."

The pair tripped across the street, but Bill wasn't watching them. As Lengers once again began walking south he fell into step beside him.

"Does the one called Gerald work with you?" Bill asked, for lack of anything else to say.

"Yes, as a window-dresser," Lengers answered, emphasizing the hyphenated word. There was an arrogant challenge in his answer, but Bill didn't rise to it.

"I suppose Shiela will be amused at your story of who you met today?"

Shiela? It took Bill a moment to realize that Lengers meant Gloria, and that he'd forgotten her name already. He swallowed the insulting remark he was going to make.

"The short one, Ross, is a chartered accountant," Lengers went on. "Groovy, eh? A gay chartered accountant, and I'll bet you thought they were all members of the Kinsmen Club and played nine holes of golf every summer Sunday?"

Bill shook his head. "No, I didn't think that," he said. "I'm not – " He formed his fingers and thumbs into a square and shoved them up into the other's face. " – as square as you think I am. I'll admit though I'm probably as naive as most people when it comes to – "

"What's your word, Willie? Fags, queers, fruits?"

"I have no special insulting name for people like you," Bill answered. "Though I guess I should have known it years ago, at the sports day in Smathers Bay."

"Suppose I told you it wasn't the only time Charley Summers and I – "

Bill laughed, "I suppose that's why he punched you and split your fucking lip!"

Lengers was about to make an angry retort, but his voice was drowned out by the roar of a couple of motorcycles that passed them, weaving in and out of the heavy slow-moving traffic.

When the noise of the bikes had lessened Bill said, "I hurried to catch up to you today because we were kids who grew up together. What either one of us has become since doesn't really matter.

"Don't pull that sympathy shit, Willie. For chrissakes, not that!"

"I don't feel any sympathy at all for you."

"Good, because I don't feel any sympathy for *you* either! Out there in your picture window split-level desert, with lovely little Shiela and the kids! God, how can you stand it!"

"Her name's Gloria," Bill said. "The sort of name you and your fag friends call yourselves when you're alone." Looking up at the garish neon sign across the facade of the building before which they'd stopped, he read it. THE CATWALK. Beneath the larger sign, above three separate doors leading into the place were signs reading, THE LIVERY STABLE, BELMONT BAR and DELMAR DINING ROOM.

A grey-haired man about Bill's height hurried out from THE LIVERY STABLE, waving a hand and looking behind him as he said goodbye to someone. He was one of them too, his hair carefully coiffured in a length that was excessive on a man of his age. He wore expensive yellow flared slacks and a Basque jersey beneath a checked sport coat.

"I'm very sorry, sir," he apologized as he turned and almost knocked Bill to the sidewalk.

"It's okay."

Bill remembered sitting with Gloria one Halloween watching a TV news segment in which men made-up to look like women and wearing women's clothes, "in drag" as they called it, stepped out of cabs and entered THE CATWALK. Crowds of people lined both sides of Y Street laughing at their exhibitionist antics, and he and Gloria had laughed too. Perhaps Tom Lengers had been one of them, as well as the polite grey-haired man who had bumped into him a moment ago. He'd wondered then, as he did now, why they chose to flaunt their aberration like that?

They hated growing old, he remembered reading somewhere. Angry now at the barbs that Lengers had thrown at him he said, "You're over the hill, Lengers. How do you attract the young ones any more? Or better still, tell me how you're going to end it all, with an overdose of barbiturates or by slashing your wrists? Those are female methods of suicide I believe."

Lengers stared at him with a homicidal hatred before he swung on his heel and entered the door leading the THE LIVERY STABLE.

Bill Bretford walked on down the street, ashamed now that his unthinking anger had made him say the things he had to Lengers. Who was he to judge the lifestyle or sexual preferences of anyone; not a psychiatrist but merely a suburban banker. He was glad life had turned out the way it had for him; other people's lives were what they'd been born with, or what their lives had made them. Perhaps Tommy had been right in his criticism of the way *he* lived too.

For the return trip north to the lot where he'd parked his car he took the subway, convincing himself it wasn't through a distaste at meeting Tommy again. The subway car was crowded: middle-aged people carrying department store paper bags, youngsters wearing their faded, patched and soiled denims, a pair of young Chinese with a cute baby in a stroller, and a white blonde girl with her arm linked with that of a bearded Black whose hair was combed out in a wild Afro halo. Bill sat rigidly in his seat reading the advertising cards until the train reached his stop.

ONE FOR THE ROAD

I seen him the minute he stepped down from the bus. He hadn't changed that much in the last nine years; still lean-looking but now kinda wanting to keep himself apart from everybody around him, telling them by the set of his mouth and jaw to leave him alone, he'd leave them alone. Not the friendly young guy that he used to be before.

A newspaperman, eh? Where from? Oh, Hamilton. No, I just wondered. That your car parked across the street? No, she'll be all right there. The plows went through here before it was light this morning.

Sure, I know Dave Tornley pretty good, same as I knew his father. Well, I don't know how it would be going out there, you'd take your own chances on that. I guess I could tell you how it was myself, or as much as I know anyways.

Coffee and a ham sandwich? Only got two kinds today, ham and salmon. Could make you a cheese I guess. Okay, ham it is.

Sure, I'll tell you how it was when Dave come home, not that there's much to it. He diden have much to say. Neither did I as far as that goes. When somebody's gone through what he went through — no, I meant in his mind more'n anything — you don't bother him any more'n you got to.

The Greyhounds only stop here in Kerrytown either to let off the odd passenger or when they're flagged. Other times they just barrel right through, either to Detroit or Toronto. The reason they take No. 2 through here, stead of sticking to the freeway, is that they usually have passengers for London. People don't believe this, but it's two miles shorter on 2 between Kerrytown and London. Of course. that's on account of the long right-angle approach to London from the freeway.

Well, sir, as I said, I seen Dave the minute he stepped down from the bus. I was outside, up to my galosh tops in snow, taking the coupla Christmas parcels from the driver, when Dave come down from the bus and headed into my store. As I said, he diden look that much different from when they took him away. He was wearing a warm gray overcoat and a peak cap but no overshoes nor rubbers.

I signed the bus driver's manifest, stepped back outa the snowbank and said, "Hello, Dave," just as he reached the door there.

For a minute he diden seem to recognize me, what with my gray hair an all, but then he said, "Hi, Mr. Potter," and come in here.

I followed him fast as I could, to get back where it was warm and to put the express parcels behind the post office counter. Then I comes along the back of the lunch counter here, and he was sitting just about where you are now.

"Can I get you somep'n, Dave?" I asks him.

"Coffee, Mr. Potter."

"Sure thing," I says.

I poured him a cup from that there old urn there, and put it in front of him. "The county bus is late," I told him. "They got a slew a snow from Port Burwell to Tillsonburg." They always do when there's a southwest wind off of Lake Erie.

He just nodded. I give him an extra container of cream.

"You fixing to go up home, Dave?" I asks him.

He nodded again, but there was no change in his face.

"The county road's good north from here," I tells him. "All the way to The Corners far as I know."

The name of the village near where the Tornley place is is really Atkinson's Corners, but nearly as long as I remember, people around these parts has just called it The Corners. I come down here from there myself as a matter of fact, after the war. That'd be in forty-eight. Bill Tornley and me — Dave's father — both seen the war through in the R.C.R's. It was a permanent force outfit that recruited around here to bring it up to strength when the war broke out. Regimental as hell, being regular army. First Div.

Well, sir, Dave just sat there sipping his coffee and looking round at the stuff on the store shelves behind you there. It was like he was catching up with things, or trying to. I went back to the post office wicket to enter up the bus parcels and finish sorting the mail — I have to send The Corners' mail the ten miles north on the county bus — and when he called me I come back out to the counter here.

"How's things up at my place?" he asks me. I guess I know what he means but I say, "I dunno, Dave. I don't go up there much no more."

"How's young Billy?" Young Bill's his son, named after his grand-dad.

"Oh, I see Billy sometimes. He's a pretty big boy now. Plays on The Corners ball team in the kids' league. Plays sometimes down here at Wamboldt Park."

He nearly smiled then. He said, "I'd better pay you, Mr. Potter, I guess." It was like not having to pay for nothing for nine years had made him forget.

"Twenty cents," I says, and his face kinda hardened, as if I was trying to take advantage of him like. I pointed up to the sign there, where he could see my posted prices. "I guess it was only a dime the last time you was here," I says. "Like most everything else it's gone up or doubled."

He pulled some folded money from his pant pocket and handed me a ten-dollar bill, that I changed for him from the post office drawer. I keep most of my folding money in the post office section of the place, cause robbing it is a federal crime and the thieves mostly get caught, even for a block of five cent stamps, an they know it.

"I was sorry to hear, well, about everything," I said to him.

"It's okay, Mr. Potter."

I wondered whether he knew everything everybody else around here knows. The things that have been happening since the murder.

"You were a friend of my father's," he said, holding his coffee cup in front of him and looking down into it.

"Yep. We joined the army together," I told him. "I diden used to see him much after the war, 'cepting when he'd drive by here in that car he bought. I guess he bought one a the first Studebakers they made after the war. What'd they call them?"

"Champion. A Studebaker Champion," he said. "He was˝pretty proud of her."

"He seemed to be pressing both hands on the coffee cup as if like to break it.

"I always found Bill to be a good man, Dave," I says.

He diden say nothing, but he nodded. I got the feeling that all the love and sorrow in his life was in that nod.

"How has things been with you these last years?" I asked him.

"Not good, Mr. Potter. Not good at all." It was as if he wanted to tell me something but diden know how. "The first couple of years were all right, but then — " He diden finish the sentence but instead drained his coffee cup.

I knew what had happened two years after he'd been put away, everybody round here knows that. I guess somebody had writ him a letter and let him know. It kinda struck me then what he'd had to face, remembering what he'd done, and then finding out it'd been the wrong thing.

"How'd the others treat you down there, Dave?" I asks him.

He put down his empty cup. "They were all right. They're a good bunch of guys, most of them," he said. "They know how these things can happen."

"I guess they give you parole?" I asked him.

"Yeah. They turned me down twice, but I finally made her."

"I'm glad, Dave," I said, reaching for his cup and saucer.

Through the front window I could see the Rev. Critchtly pulling his Chevy into the curb, clean between the NO PARKING – BUS STOP signs. I went around the counter here to the door and waved to Critchtly to get parked legal. His fat wife opened the car's window on her side and said in her high-falutin social service kinda voice, "I'm only dropping in for our mail. We'll be out of here before a bus comes."

"I'm expecting the Middlesex County bus any minute."

She opened the car door and comes towards me, not paying no attention to what I'd said. I shut the front door there in her face and comes back to the lunch counter.

"Could you stand another coffee, Dave?" I asked him. Through a corner of my eye I could see the minister's wife come through the front door and stand up against the mail wicket. I paid no attention at all.

"Dave," I said, sorta waking him from his thoughts. He was staring down at the counter.

"Eh?"

"Do you want another coffee, Dave?" I asks him.

He looks up at the price sign, kinda half smiled and shook his head.

"It'll be on the house, Dave," I said. "No charge. Have another one for the road."

After a minute he says, "Okay, Mr. Potter." And then, "Thanks."

I guess he hadn't had much to thank anybody for for a long time.

I drew another coffee from the urn and give it to him, with two creams. It wasn't that much, I know, but like I was the only one to meet him you might say, and his father and me had been sorta regimental close. Not buddies exactly but in the same outfit.

When I'd fixed him up, an he was spooning in his sugar, I went along to the post office there and took the Critchtly's mail from its slot and handed it to Critchtly's wife.

She's one a them women around here that has to sort their mail again at the wicket. She always says, "Junk mail an bills, that's all we get these days."

"Your husband's cheque is there too," I says.

"How do *you* know that?" she asks me, trying to look — yeah, haughty I guess it is. Stuck up. She's one woman can't do it on account of the fat on her face.

"It's my job to know what mail I get," I says. "I can recognize a cheque from a bill, and I can tell the pension cheques from the baby bonus. I knew that was your husband's cheque from the church office in Toronto right off. Why even holding services in two churches every Sunday he'd have to leave these parts if the head office diden pay his wages."

Being a preacher these days is like being a harness maker. Critchtly does a Sunday morning service here at St. John's and then a service after supper at St. Jude's up at The Corners. Between the two a them his congregation wouldn't fill ten pews. The head office has made them both mission churches or somep'n, and they pay Critchtly's wages.

Mrs. Critchtly scooped up their mail and turned around to leave, and I guess that's when she noticed Dave Tornley sitting there at the counter.

"You — you're *out!*" she yelled, pressing the handful of mail against her for protection or something.

Dave looked at her then, for the first time since she'd come in, I guess.

"Yeh, Mz. Critchtly, I'm out," Dave says. I swear he hadn't no expression on his face at all. Nothing. "I got your letters," he says. "I never answered none of them, but I read them all. I sure as hell read them all."

I knew now who it was had told him everything had happened. Imagine, him locked up down there in Kingston, not able to get out and do nothing, feeling like he must of about what had happened, and old lady Critchtly writing him regular telling him things he didn't want to know, just rubbing it all in like salt on an open sore. Honest to gawd I

145

wished right then I'd of tore up Critchtly's pay cheque, federal offence or not.

Old lady Critchtly – she's really younger'n me but the kinda woman you sort of always thought of as old – well, sir, she run right out of the door there without shutting it behind her. She wouldn't of been long in jumping into Critchtly's car neither, but she couldn't.

What kind of pie. We got apple and raisin today. Apple? An another coffee? Okay.

Why? Oh you mean about the Critchtlys? Well, sir, it was funnier'n hell. Just then the county bus pulls in, and McComb the driver gives old man Critchtly a blast a the horn that'd scared the bejeezus outa Joshua himself. Critchtly, that's still got his Chevy in gear, shoves her forward right into about five feet of soft snow I'd piled up from the sidewalk in front of my place. He dug into her nearly back to the windshield. His wife's running up and down shouting at him, but Critchtly can't back up none even if he could on account of the front of McComb's bus is touching his rear bumper. Critchtly tries to ram his old car through the snow pile but he can't on account of how deep it was and besides he's got his front wheels turned out the roadway.

I watched Critchtly for a minute while McComb was letting off a Kerrytown woman that's a chambermaid mornings at a motel just north of the freeway. McComb comes in, stamping the snow off of his rubbers, and hands me a parcel for London. While I'm checking and signing the manifest both of us is listening to Critchtly tearing the guts outa his car.

"What'd he want to park at the bus sign for?" McComb asks me.

"I dunno, Jim. I guess his wife thinks that cause he wears that white dog collar he can park just about anywheres he wants. I told him I was expecting you any minute."

McComb asks me, "Anything for The Corners?"

"No express. Got a passenger for you though." I point over here to the lunch counter.

McComb looks over at Dave Tornley, sorta starts like, looks at me and then walks over to Dave.

"Hello, Dave," he says. "Glad to see you again."

Dave looks back at him for a long time, just eyeing him like. Then he sticks out his hand. "Hello, Jim," he says. "You're still on the bus,

146

eh?"

"Yep," McComb says, nervous like. He shakes Tornley's hand. "Another year to go to my pension. Twenty-seven years now." I seen McComb grin then for maybe the second time since I known him. "It beats all hell how time flies."

Dave just stares him down.

"Sorry, Dave, I didn't mean that," McComb says. "You got any luggage, Dave?"

I'd never heard McComb ask no passenger, man nor woman, about luggage before. It made me certain about him, as I'd been certain about some others I could name for a long time.

Dave said, "All I got is what I'm wearing."

"Okay, let's go then," McComb says, leading the way to the front door.

When the door was opened you could hear old Critchtly stripping his gears with a sound like a reaper hitting a rockpile. His missus was up to her fat waist in snow trying to pull open the car door.

"Thanks, Mr. Potter," Dave said, shaking my hand before following McComb out to the bus. "It was good of you to give me that second cup of coffee."

"It's nothing," I told him.

"One for the road, eh?" he said, coming as close as he ever could any more to a smile, I guess. I watched him climbing the steps to the bus.

To tell you the truth I didn't know what to think after Dave had gone. I had some crazy ideas, let me tell you, after he'd left.

After the bus pulled out and the Critchtly's car was quiet, Critchtly's wife come back in here and walked over to the store side. She hefted one of them snow shovels over there against the wall, first one of them steel ones then an aluminum.

"May I borrow one of these shovels for a moment, Mr. Potter?" she asks me.

I never even knew before that she even knew my name.

"Nope," I told her. "They're for sale not lend. The steel ones is three-ninety-five and the aluminum four-eighty-five, without counting the tax."

"What about the one you use yourself then?" she asks.

147

I walked over to that there window there and looked out at their car. "What you need now, I'd say, is a tow truck. You might be able to get Scotty Morrison's over at the Shell station."

"That's away over past the other end of town," she says.

"Yep."

She give me a look then meant to damn me to her husband's hellfire. I'd a let her phone Scotty's, but she was outa that door like a shot, slamming it so hard behind her that that little bell kept ringing a long time after she'd gone.

I went back into our kitchen there and told my wife Viola that Dave Tornley was out on parole, and had just left on the county bus for The Corners. "Maybe I should phone the Provincial Police detachment," I said. "The way Dave looked when he left here we don't know what might happen when he gets home. I wouldn't want him to do nothing crazy."

"I've known Davey since he was a little boy playing with our Bobby," Viola said. "He won't do nothing crazy. It's you what's crazy, Gerald Potter, wanting to do a fool thing like phoning the police."

I kinda knew she was prolly right, an mad too, 'cause that's the only time she calls me by my full name.

"How'd he look?" she asks me.

"Same as ever I guess. Nine years older but he hasn't changed that much."

"Whyn't you call me out to say hello to him?" she asks me. "You knew I always liked young Dave, and that I didn't blame him none for what he did."

"I should've, I guess, Vi. I just forgot," I said, getting back here out of her kitchen.

The county bus was late getting back here, and McComb just slowed her down enough out in front so I could give him a highball that there's no passengers going south. I really don't know what happened at the Tornley place, but later on, from a farmer from down near Springford that had gone up to The Corners in the same bus as Dave, I found out that after McComb had let the farmer out he'd turned the bus east on the concession road towards the Tornley place. I don't know whether Dave had asked him to or made him or whether it was McComb's idea. In the accomodating way McComb had acted to Dave when he met him

148

here it could have been either of them. Anyways, though I didn't see them in the bus when McComb slowed her down on his way back I found out later that he'd driven Dave's wife Mabel and her two youngest children through to Tillsonburg.

That's where she come from before her and Dave was married. She was one a the Kroetch girls from down there; her father's got a tobacco farm. The kids and her is living down there now.

Yes, she had three kiddies, but only her and the two youngest are living at her father's. Dave kept young Billy up at his place with him. Well, it seems pretty dang natural to me. Billy was the only one of them that Dave could be half sure of was his own. The second one wasn't born till Dave had been put away for two years, so no way could it have been his. The smallest one neither. Billy's named after his grand-dad, and I guess he's the only thing Dave's got any more.

By golly my wife was right too about phoning the police. *I* didn't need to 'cause the Critchtly woman beat me to it. 'Stead of phoning for Scotty Morrison's tow truck she stopped in the Rexall down the street and phoned the Provincials from the phone booth there. It's not that funny but I gotta laugh when I think of how she left old Critchtly freezin to death out there in his stuck car. Maybe it *was* heartless, but there's them I'd do anything for and them I'd do nothing for.

Dave let Mabel dress the kids up warm and throw some things in a suitcase before he put her on McComb's bus. That I got from one a the Provincials that went up to the Tornley place after the preacher's wife phoned them to send a squad car. What could the police do to Dave, unless he did something crazy? After all, old Bill Tornley's farm is now his, ain't it?

A few days after Dave come home, McComb come in here on one of his southbound trips from The Corners. He was kinda limping, and when I asked him what was the matter he opened his luggage and express compartment and showed me two great big cardboard cartons he'd picked up at The Corners for Tillsonburg.

"They're Mabel's things," he said, and I knew then I'd been right about McComb and Dave's wife. Not that he was the only one of course. "That son of a bitch Tornley made me carry them from his car trunk an load them into my bus myself," he said. "They nearly give me a rupture."

So far as I know Dave and young Billy is living at the farm. He has a Mrs. Cregar that lives in the village go out and do the washing and things once in a while. He sold sixty acres of the land along the road, and they tell me he's trying to start another dairy herd like Bill Tornley used to have. Holsteins now, not the registered Guernseys old Bill had. Mabel practically give the herd away after Dave went to prison. Let the house an buildings go to rack an ruin too. Crops? She didn't grow no crops! The only crop she sold was the one she was born with, and mostly she give that away.

Let's see, I guess Mabel's twenty-eight or so now. Dave's maybe thirty-one. He was twenty-two at the time of the murder and I guess Mabel was around nineteen. There'd been others before but Dave hadn't know about them. Of course Dave thought it was his wife that was being raped, not the other way round. I still think he'd of got off with less than murder if he'd a had a better lawyer than that there Woolsley. Well the judge down in London — Yeah, Bramshott, that died last year. He had it figured wrong, and so did the jury. No, sir, Dave didn't say nothing in court. I was there the day he got sentenced, and I think he'd been happier to be hung.

It must have been plain hell for him down in the pen. 'Specially after that old bitch Mrs. Critchtly writ him about Mabel's carrying on and about the other babies. Like here was a poor guy thinking and thinking about the awful thing he'd done, and then he finds out that though it was still awful it wasn't really the fault of the one he'd killed, but that it was his wife's fault. He's stuck now with two different lines of thought, both of them awful but one kinda contradicting the other. Now that he knew the truth it made the murder fifty times harder to take. Imagine nine years of that!

I'm sure glad Dave and the Critchtly woman met each other right in here. If it hadn't been for that I'd never have known who it was that writ him. Damn it, I might tear up one of Critchtly's pay cheques yet!

Nope, Dave ain't been in here since the day he come home. I've seen him a coupla times when he passes in his car. He always gives me a wave.

You can go out if you want to, but I don't think it'd be smart to go out there an try to talk to him. They tell me he's got this police dog he bought in London, a trained guard dog. Some guy called Gurton or Gurney or somep'n like that, from up Ingersoll way, drove into the Tornley yard. The guy didn't know Mabel had gone an Dave was living there. I guess the dog like to tear the leg off him before Dave called him off.

'You say you still think it'd make a good story? Maybe your paper's got some readers that like reading about a young boy shooting his own father when he finds him in bed with his young wife. I guess to them kind any story like that is news, even if it's nine years old. You can write it if you've a mind to, but what else could you learn from talking to Dave Tornley? I've told you the whole thing myself. If you can't write it like I told it to you, you ain't much of a writer is all I can say.

Let's see, two coffees, a lettuce-'n-ham sandwich, an a slice of Mrs. Potter's homemade apple pie. That'll be forty, one-ten, one-forty-five. Take a look up at the price board there. It'd cost you more'n that in Hamilton, and the pie'd be made in a factory. Besides, you wouldn't a learned what you did about what the papers called The Shotgun Patricide.

Here's your change, an don't forget that thin suitcase of yours. An attache case? I guess all you younger newspapermen carry them things now?

Drop in again the next time you're down this way.

No, Vi, he's from Hamilton he says. See, he's making a U-turn. He's changed his mind about going up to bother Dave. I guess it was the lie I told him about Dave Tornley's guard dog. It's better to tell a white lie to somebody like that than let them tell a bunch a black lies in their newspaper.

151

A SHORT WALK HOME

Linda and Penny didn't leave the concert until well after the drawn-out terminal chord had been strung and riffed by the final group on the bill, The Barbarian Horde. Then Penny had insisted they wait at the performers' entrance, which wasn't that so much as an old warehouse shipping door, till she'd got Dinty Driscoe's autograph.

Penny had finally got Driscoe to scribble his name on the back of her Xeroxed souvenir program, after they'd waited nearly an hour for the group to emerge from the hall and climb into their Volkswagen bus.

Linda had been forced to wait for her friend, not only peevishly impatient with Penny but scared too of what her parents would say this time about her being late again. *She* didn't want any of the musicians' autographs at all, not even Rick Blamey's. And she certainly wasn't interested in Driscoe, who was only the bass guitarist of the group. Several times she tugged at Penny's arm, insisting they'd miss the last bus home from the subway station. She didn't want another hassle with her old lady about the hours she was keeping, listening once again to, "Nothing good'll happen to any girl that stays out half the night, you mark my words, young lady!"

Sometimes she hated her parents as much as she did the other creeps of their generation, and often envied young Eleanor Billings who'd had to get married and now lived with her baby and husband down here in the city drawing Welfare. At least Eleanor was doing her own thing. Just wait till she too could legally leave home, in a few months time, she'd leave too, maybe hitching out to the Coast like Joan and Barb had done the previous summer.

Despite her nagging she'd waited for Penny, the older girl's patience beating down her own fearful urge to leave as it always did, conceding the fact that Penny was the dominant member of the pair. It wasn't only that her girl friend was seventeen against her own stupid fifteen and a half, but because Penny had more freedom than she'd ever had, living in a fatherless home and everything.

Still, the wait for the autograph was kind of fun in a way, standing together in the laneway behind The Rock Pile, as the converted warehouse was named, listening to the chatter of the younger screechies and watching the older ones, already women really, who stood apart from the younger kids trying to look bored and sophisticated in their hip-widened jeans and thrust-out sweaters. She knew, from Penny mostly who'd been going to rock concerts and festivals since she was twelve, that these older women who still cracked their gum and called each other "girls" were left-over groupies. Listening to bits of their conversations she knew they couldn't forget those earlier years they called "the big time."

The wait in the alley was good for a couple of other things too: it let her see that the musicians in the rock bands, not only The Barbarian Horde which had been the top attraction, but the others from The Signal Tower and Speed Kills, were really nothing at all without the strobe lights, stage glitter, their instruments and the screaming crowd. Most of them in their street clothes had no more personality or sexual attraction than the Grade Ten kids at General Wilson High. They were younger too than they looked on stage. Letting themselves be bullied and cursed at by older and shorter creeps with too-long sideburns for their age and sport jackets whose flaps didn't quite meet at the back. The other thing the wait was good for was that it supplied her and Penny things to talk about on their way home. There weren't many things they could really rap on about the concert itself. All either of them knew about the music and even the group leaders' names had been culled from the papers, school conversations and disk-jockey shows.

On the subway Penny tried to imitate Carole King singing *Fantasy*, but only sounded like a third-hand imitation of Anne Murray. Now, since boarding the Fairview Hills bus, they talked mainly about what they'd seen and heard after the cheap little traveling rock concert was over. Things like the words Dumpy Ford, the drummer from Speed Kills, had used when a piece of his equipment got jammed in the door of his beat-up Cutlass. And the question Driscoe had put to the overpainted old groupie who had come up to him just after he'd handed back Penny's program with a hurried "thank ya" and an out-of-it smile. Penny explained what the slang expression meant. It had really shook Linda that one of their own young gods would ask a strange woman something like that, and shook her more that the woman smiled her acceptance and jumped into the Volks bus with him.

When they mentioned Garry Archambault, who played lead guitar and did most of the vocals for The Signal Tower, unbuttoning his rhinestoned purple velvet shirt in a strip-tease that got them all going, an old woman sitting in front of them turned around and gave them her old creep's disapproving stare. Penny stuck her tongue out at her, so that the old woman jerked her head around and concentrated on the overloaded shopping bag she held on her lap. The old creep reminded Linda of her Grandma Foster whom she'd been forced to visit in the nursing home till she'd died, and who always talked to her in baby talk that wasn't even funny but only crazy boring.

"That Garry's hairy chest turned me on," Penny said, speaking to Linda but loud enough for the old woman to hear. Lowering her voice just a bit so the old creep had to strain to listen-in she went on, "I can feel it now, rubbing on . . . " Nudging Linda as she let the sentence trail off into nothing. It was a game they sometimes played in crowds when they knew some drip was tuned in.

The bus, which had left the subway station with standees, was half empty by the time it reached Marlborough, and at the next stop, Airport Avenue, the old woman with her shopping bag got off. She first turned her head and gave the two girls a disgusted sniff that sent them into a fit of giggling and caused some of the other passengers to look around.

Her mother didn't want her to go around with Penny, not only because of what she called Penny's homelife but also she thought Penny was too sophisticated for her age. Not that Mrs. Grainford ever used the word "sophisticated," but instead substituted phrases like "too forward" or "a little snit," and had once called Penny "A silly teenage flirt that'll get what's coming to her some day." Nothing she'd said had been enough to keep the girls apart.

Without the older Penny, whose difference in age, she had to admit, was a lot more than the span in their birthdates, Linda knew she'd have remained as dumb as her cousin Maureen. Her mother was always throwing her niece at her as an example of a perfect young lady. For herself, she'd sooner be dead than as stupid as her Aunt Vera had brought Maureen up to be!

She knew better than her mother what Penny was, and she wasn't stupid enough not to know that most of it was just put on or was a bragging exaggeration of the real Penny. Sometimes though her friend made her sick with her clumsy attempts to hide things Linda already knew or sensed.

'Watch that kinky bus-driver, Linda," Penny said.

"What?"

"The bus driver. See him in his mirror?"

"Yeah. What of it?"

"He's been staring at me every chance he gets since we laughed at the old creep with the shopping bag. I think I got him going."

Penny was always saying such things about any man who looked at her. Linda thought it was because Penny's father had deserted her and her mother years before. She'd said this once to her own mother when they were having a usual hassle about her girl friend.

"Mmmph!" her mother had snorted.

"Why not? It's like in psychology. It's what they call a search for a surrogate father."

"Listen, young lady, I don't need to hear about psychology," her mother had thrown over her shoulder. "It's not psychology that's wrong with Penny Grenfell, Miss know-it-all."

Linda thought, what else could she expect from a middle-aged woman who thought nothing had changed since 1950, and that skirts shouldn't be worn higher than two inches above the knee. Her mother was smart enough in some ways but not much of an expert in the way things were today. And she was absolutely dumb about sex, except knowing it didn't happen in broad daylight on a well-traveled street.

"You think I can't tell?" Penny asked, jarring Linda out of her thoughts.

"Eh? Oh I guess so, Penny."

"You think I haven't gone all the way with a man?"

"I know," Linda said.

This was another thing that made Penny the acknowledged leader of the pair. Linda had heard different versions of the story a half dozen times. Penny claimed it had happened when she was fourteen and living downtown. The man's name had been George, sometimes a boarder in their house while at others her mother's boy friend.

The way Penny told it, one Saturday morning after her mother had gone to work at the downtown department store she still worked at, George (no matter what version she told, his name didn't change) had climbed into Penny's bed and had either seduced her or had "played around" with her, depending on which version she told. If it was the latter, he'd seduced her later on.

The first time she'd heard it Penny's story had been horrible and exciting, but later it only bored or depressed Linda. What it constantly did was make her envy Penny's sophistication, a word she'd been using more and more lately. Tonight the reminder of George, real or not, only bored her, along with the bus driver's imagined stares.

Usually her father waited in the car for them at the plaza parking lot, but she'd seldom been *this* late before. He'd probably have driven home long before as he'd done on another occasion, only having come at her mother's insistence. He'd always allowed her mother to run him as she still tried to run her children, even Dorothy who'd been married now for two years.

Most of the remaining passengers got off at Fairhaven Road, the last stop before the bus turned around at the shopping plaza. This left only Linda, Penny and a young man with black curly hair who was sitting behind the driver. The driver removed his cap from his bald head, shook a cigarette pack and lighted it, and let its smoke curl up to the SMOK-ING PROHIBITED sign above the double windshields. He gave a challenging glace at his passengers through his internal rewr-view mirror, but none of them paid him any attention. So much for Penny's imagined flirtation.

Linda made up her mind to tell the truth of having to wait for Penny to get her autograph, leaving out any mention of the aging groupies. Mentioning them would only give her mother — and her father too who would have had to stay up after the late news at her mother's nagging insistence — to predict the same end for *her* if she didn't get her mind off rock music and stop going around with Penny Grenfell.

When the bus pulled into the end-of-the-line stop at the plaza Penny jumped down first. When Linda alighted she was followed closely by the sole male passenger. He looked a little familiar, like someone she'd seen only occasionally before; shy and scared-looking, in his early twenties. Just as she stepped out to catch up with Penny she thought she heard him mumble, "Wanna make it, baby?" When she looked around he was heading around the group who were waiting to board the bus. He didn't look around at her, and she dismissed him as some kind of Fairview Hills creep.

157

On their way across the parking lot to where Linda's father usually parked, the girls argued whether Paul Simon's singing of *Kodachrome* was better than George Harrison's *Give Me Love*. This inconclusive uninformed spat reminded Penny of a "fabulous" cassette offer she'd heard on the local rock station that morning. By the time they were certain that the parking lot was empty of the Grainford's car, Penny said, "Come on, Linda, it's only a short walk home." By the time they headed up Hawthorne, their conversation had swung back to reminiscing about the events of the evening.

Linda said, "You know, Pen, I really hated those old groupie women outside The Rock Pile tonight. Imagine them living on the hope they'll be picked up again by those kids in the bands."

"How about the one Dinty Driscoe picked up?"

"Sure. A filthy old slut who'd even do *that* for a young celebrity."

Penny laughed. "Gawd, you're innocent, Linda." She shrugged. "It's their life. I guess most of them have had their couple of years at the top, traveling everywhere with a group, being the girl of somebody big maybe, hitting it high. It's more than they could have got from working in a crummy office and then marrying some jerk that's learned to string tape through a computer. Then ending up out here in Diaperville."

After a long moment or two Linda asked, "I wonder what *we'll* be doing at their age, Penny?"

Her friend laughed. "I don't know and don't care. Who knows, maybe I'll be living with Garry Archambault and his bee-u-ti-ful scratchy chest." A would-be carefree laugh. "Maybe I'll be married to some guy that strings computers for IBM instead of a gee-tar for Speed Kills."

Linda playfully pushed Penny into a lawn hedge, and both girls ran along the suburban sidewalk, screeching with laughter and causing a far-off dog to bark.

About a half block ahead of them, going in their direction and just crossing Beardmore, was the drunkenly staggering figure of a short fat man.

"The bars must be closed," said Penny, who noticed him first.

"It's that old juice head, Jennifer Alcott's father, heading home from the Legion Hall," Linda said.

"Let's tease the old twirp," Linda proposed, giggling.

"Not *me*," said Linda. Then vehemently, "I've hated him ever since I called for Jenny, and he came to the door and said she wasn't in. The creepy old liar! I could see Jenny through their kitchen doorway. It was him and her old lady, I *know*, that stopped Jenny from even walking home from school with me. Let's cross to the opposite sidewalk till we're past him."

They did so, not re-crossing the street until they were at least a block ahead of the drunken man. For once they said a quick goodnight in front of Penny's apartment building. When she left her friend, Linda looked back and saw that old man Alcott was at least two blocks behind her.

Linda hurried along Hawthorne towards Maplelea, frightendly aware of the deserted loneliness of the late-night quiet of the neighborhood, her apprehensiveness shoving her coming confrontation with her parents to the back of her mind.

Near the corner of Hawthorne and Maplelea was a small shallow stream crossed by a low-walled culvert. Below the surface of the street the stream became an underground storm sewer making it way under the city. It was blocked off at its entrance by a locked heavy wire gate to prevent small children or heavy debris from being carried into the sewage system.

As Linda hurried past the far end of the low culvert wall she heard a movement behind her, and a strong thin dirty hand was clamped over her mouth while the other clutched her by a breast and dragged her backwards into the muddy hollow carved by the stream. In her struggles to tear her attacker's hand from her mouth her bag slipped from her shoulder to the sidewalk.

All her imagined reactions to such an occurrence were lost in the suddenness of the attack, so that she could neither grasp or kick her attacker. She was thrown to the ground, the hand released her breast, and she both heard and felt the metallic unzipping of her jeans and the nylon tear of her underthings. She tried to cry out into the hand that covered her mouth but could not. With the dirty hand still pressed against her clenched teeth she felt a man's uncovered body pressing down on hers and heard his heavy breathing against her throat. Then

159

her head began spinning faster and faster as she was carried into the vortex of an approaching blackness . . . .

When she came to and tried to struggle to her feet she realized she was still lying in the muddy grass at the side of the narrow gurgling stream. There were two men in blue police caps and uniform shirts standing over her, and on the street she caught a glimpse of the unlighted dome of a police car. A policeman holding her bag in his hand was staring down at her, and suddenly conscious of her nakedness she pulled down her sweater and groped for her jeans that were bunched around an ankle.

"Take it easy, Miss," said the policeman who was holding her bag.

A drunken face appeared, and she recognized old man Alcott lying nearby in the grass.

"No!" she screamed. "Get him away from me!"

"Hey, listen — " the drunk began, before the second policeman knocked him back out of sight. She could hear Alcott's drunken protests as the policeman holding her purse asked, "Where do you live, Miss?"

"Eighteen Maplelea," she answered.

The other policeman pulled old man Alcott up by his hair and asked her, "Do you know this man?"

She stared into Alcott's incredulous quickly-sobering eyes and nodded.

"Listen, officers, sure she knows me. I live on Maplelea myself, only a block or so from her," Alcott said. "She goes to General Wilson High along with my daughter Jennifer. Isn't that right, Miss — Miss — "

Somehow she'd managed to pull up her jeans and tuck in her sweater. The policeman handed her her draw-string tote bag with its long buckled strap.

"Is what he says right, Miss?"

She nodded.

The other policeman pulled Alcott, swaying tipsily, to his feet. The policeman had the man's wallet in his hand, looking through it with his flashlight. In the light Linda saw that old man Alcott's feet and the bottoms of his pantlegs were wet. She tore her eyes off him when she noticed that the front of his trousers gaped open.

"Zipper yourself up, you," a policeman ordered him.

As if unaware of it before, Alcott turned from her and closed his fly.

"You know his daughter?" the policeman asked her.

"I – " She nodded again. She felt she was about to faint, and grabbed the policeman's sleeve to keep herself from falling.

The second one said, "I'll take him down to the station, Bill, and have another car pick up you two and her father or mother. Is your father home, Miss?"

She nodded.

Old man Alcott pleaded, "Listen, there's been a mistake. I didn't do anything to this little girl, as God's my judge! She knows it wasn't me."

"Come on," the policeman ordered, roughly pulling Alcott up to the sidewalk.

Linda and the other officer reached the sidewalk in time to watch the car drive off. The policeman at the wheel signalled that he'd radioed for another car. Old man Alcott's hands waved wildly as he said something to the driver.

"Maybe you'd better sit down, Miss," the other one said, and she seated herself on the culvert parapet. The policeman glanced at his watch in the light from a nearby street lamp and began writing in his notebook. She gave him her name and address.

A second police car came up Hawthorne with its red light flashing, and she was helped into the back seat. After a whispered conversation between the policeman who'd found her and the driver's partner they turned up Maplelea and stopped in front of her house.

When she opened the front door her father advanced across the living room his mouth opened ready to bawl her out. It closed though as both he and her mother, who was close behind him, saw the young policeman. They were hurriedly ushered indoors out of sight of the neighbors. Her father asked what had happened.

"Well, Mr. – " He consulted his notebook. "Mr. Grainford, your daughter has been attacked."

"Attacked!" her mother screamed, placing the back of her hand against her mouth and stepping back to get a better look at Linda.

"How do you mean, Officer, attacked?" her father asked. He sounded every inch what he was, the housing development supervisor asking a new mortgagee what he meant by saying his basement drain was backing up.

Linda giggled. She felt a queer enjoyment in seeing her parents like this.

The policeman stared at her strangely then said, "Maybe she can tell you better than *I* can."

Her father asked, "Did you have your purse snatched, dear, or what?"

In answer she swung her tote bag by its strap. She was aware that it was the first time since her early childhood that her father had called her "dear." She was aware too that the young policeman had removed his cap, and that his heavy polished boots were spattered with mud.

The policeman said, "My partner and I were making a routine cruise around the streets of Westbury Hills, sir. My partner, Constable James McNichol, observed this young lady's bag lying on the north sidewalk of Hawthorne Road, around the corner from Maplelea Boulevard, in the vicinity of the spot where Fuller's Creek runs under Hawthorne and becomes – "

"Her bag on the sidewalk? Yes, yes, go on!" urged her father.

It's like a TV show, Linda thought, where the arresting officer uses police jargon when reading from his notebook to the judge and jury. She had to stifle another urge to giggle.

The policeman went on, punctuating his story with words like "investigation," "evidence," and "suspect," the gist of which was that Linda had been lying, her clothing disarranged and obviously in a faint . . . .

"Oh, my lord!" Mrs. Grainford cried, looking Linda over for visible signs of sexual disobedience.

"Kneeling beside the girl was the figure of a man, since removed to No. 42 Division police station as a suspect – "

"A suspect! You mean you found a man kneeling beside my stripped and unconscious little girl and you only take him in as a *suspect*?"

"He hasn't been tried yet, Mr. Grainford." The young policeman's voice had an edge to it, as if her father was an old hated schoolteacher who was trying to jolly himself out of a traffic citation.

"Yes, yes, I see."

"Your daughter wasn't *completely* stripped either," the policeman said to her mother, who was whining behind her hand. Linda felt she was getting even with all the old creeps who had run her life up to then.

"Who was the man the officers found, Linda?"

She shrugged.

The policeman read from his notebook. "William Alcott."

Her mother found her voice, and squeaked, "The Alcotts up the street, past Waterdown? Jennifer's father?"

Her father's mouth hung open.

The policeman said that Linda and her father would have to come down to the station, where she could give preliminary evidence against the accused. First though she'd have to undergo a routine medical examination at the Westbury Hills General.

The young interne in the emergency ward at the hospital treated the examination as a sort of joke, and actually winked at her when it was over. The confrontation with old man Alcott was far more serious, with the now sober Alcott threatening them all with false arrest suits and staring right through Linda so that she burst into tears and cried, "Take him away from me! Please!"

By the time he was formally charged Alcott had sunk into a disbelieving quiet, and didn't even look at her as he was led away to the cells. As for Linda it was the first time in her life it was she who was listened to and treated with respect.

Late the following morning, a Saturday, she was relentlessly questioned, in the presence of a uniformed policewoman, by a senior plainclothes police officer with a grey crew-cut. She hated him on sight, and his questions made her feel *she* was the accused.

His interrogation was a tricky crossword of confusing questions, which she answered either in monosyllables or with an angered pout.

Had she known the accused before? Had she ever walked home with him? Did she get a look at her attacker's face? At what he was wearing? Had she or Penny spoken to anyone else after getting off the bus at the Playland Plaza? Had either of them spoken to anyone *on* the bus? Had she been conscious of anyone following them? All right, they'd crossed the street to avoid having to pass an obviously drunken William Alcott. She and Penny had then recrossed the street? Where? How far back was Alcott then? Had she looked back after leaving Penny? Where was Alcott then? Maybe a block? How far is a block? Had Alcott appeared to be hurrying? No, *after* she'd left Penny. And she'd met no-one, not even a woman or a child? And no cars had passed her, in either direction, on Hawthorne? Or on one of the cross streets? Exactly how far back was Alcott when she left Penny at her apartment house? She'd said a block a few minutes ago. How long, in her estimation of the speed he was walking — ? What, running? All right, staggering then — how long would it have taken him to catch up to her?

She began to cry and the old creep merely handed her a Kleenex. After she'd blown her nose but before she could take the tissue from her eyes the questions continued.

Did her attacker threaten her with anything? Did he have a gun? A knife? A club? Did he choke her? Threaten to? Threaten to kill her in any other way? Did he imply that he'd kill her or cause her bodily harm unless she submitted to him? Did she infer from *any* action of his that it was his intention to do so? Was she afraid he might murder her *after* committing the act? Could she have screamed during the time the act was taking place? Before? After? What was the hand over her mouth like? Old? Gnarled? Thin? Fat? Did it taste or smell of anything? Well, like hand lotion? Soap? Gas or oil? Spaghetti sauce? Beer?

Did her attacker say *anything* to her? Was he light, heavy, fat, thin, hairy? She'd felt him pressing down on her hadn't she? But then she'd fainted? I see, just *when* had she fainted, before, during or after the act took place? Had she known any other girls in Fairview Hills to be attacked? Any girls at school? What about Penny Grenfell? Yes, that had been different, but had it made her envious of her friend?

No, no, no, no, NO! More tears, another Kleenex.

Coming back to Alcott again, would she expect any man she knew as well as she knew Alcott *not* to kill her to protect himself? According to the arresting officers he'd known who *she* was, so he must have known she also knew *him*. Would she have expected any man in the neighborhood to ignore the sight of a stripped and unconscious — maybe dead — young girl? Wouldn't she have expected her own father to have stopped and tried to help? Wasn't it possible, as he claimed, that Alcott had gone down the opposite bank of the creek beside the culvert to relieve himself, and seeing her lying there had waded through the shallow water to give her help? They knew that was the way he'd reached her side, for they'd found his footprints down the opposite bank. Wouldn't the shock of finding her lying there, to a man in Alcott's condition at the time, be more important to him than zipping up his trousers?

He tossed her the box of Kleenex.

How long had she known the Alcotts? Was Jennifer Alcott an old friend? An acquaintance? No friend at all? Why, had they once quarrelled? How about Mr. or Mrs. Alcott? Had he every spoken to her? When was that? A year or so before, and he'd just told her Jenny wasn't in? I see. How about other men she knew? All right, boys then? Schoolmates? Boy friends? Ex-boy friends?

So she'd fainted without recognizing her attacker? And so she wasn't absolutely sure it *had* been William Alcott? . . . The questions went on and on . . . Her friend Penny claimed that Alcott was too far behind them on Hawthorne to have caught up with her. Unless she'd waited for him, of course? . . . No, no, no, no, NO! She jumped up from her chair.

Okay, Miss Grainford, I just hope you realize what a serious charge rape is, and what it will mean to the Alcott family? Also, your attacker, presuming it *wasn't* Alcott, is still free to attack you or any other young girl again. You know that.

She shook her head.

The old creep swivelled his chair so that his back was to her, and said to the policewoman, "All right, officer, take her back to her father. They can go."

William Alcott, unable on a weekend to raise the necessary bail on such a serious charge, was transferred from the police station to the city jail on Saturday afternoon. His body was found at approximately 4:10 a.m. the following morning, hanging with one sleeve of his shirt knotted around his neck and the other sleeve knotted around a high horizontal bar of his cell. Cause of death, self-inflicted strangulation.

The newspapers ignored both the rape and Alcott's suicide, and hardly anyone knew anything about either. The Grainford's family doctor put her on tranquilizers, and she slept quite a lot and between times watched television. Penny called her up several times, and a couple of weeks after the attack came to see her. After her mother had

left the house to go to the shopping plaza Linda told her friend everything she remembered until she'd fainted, and Penny took it all in
eagerly, asking her for every little detail. When she got up to leave,
Penny said, "I wonder who it could have been?"

"Old man Alcott of course, who else!" Linda answered angrily.

"Oh, Linda, come on!"

Penny called her up a couple of times after that, but Linda refused
to talk to her.

One evening Mrs. Alcott called at the house, and Linda, who was in
the kitchen at the time, ran into her room and held the door shut.
After Mrs. Alcott had gone both her parents remarked on what a nice
woman Mrs. Alcott was. Her mother said she'd told them Linda had
made a terrible mistake accusing a good man − "a good husband and
father," her actual words had been − but she didn't hold it against
her.

By the time school opened in the fall Mrs. Alcott had sold her house
and moved away with her children. Penny didn't return to General
Wilson High but took up with a young poet and song lyricist and moved
down to the city again. Linda's rape and Alcott's suicide had seemingly
been forgotten by the few who had ever known of them, so that it
seemed to Linda they hadn't happened at all. She began going steady
with a boy named Arthur Luncey in Grade Twelve. They shared a
liking for rock music, and traded cassettes and things, but they didn't
attend as many rock concerts as she and Penny had done.

One evening in early December, after Mr. and Mrs. Grainford had
left the house to catch the early movie at the plaza, Linda heard Arthur's knock on the door. He was a half hour early and she still had her
hair in curlers, so she was angry with him when she opened the door.
She didn't want him to see her hair in that state so she turned and
crossed the living room as he entered the house and shut the door
behind him.

"Hy, Linda," he said, and something strange but familiar in his
voice made her swing around and face him.

It wasn't Arthur at all, but the young man who had followed her out
of the bus that terrible night in the summer. Still seemingly afraid
and shy he kept his eyes on the rug. She now recognized him as the
dark-haired young man who worked at the vegetable counter down at

the supermarket. Though he didn't look at her she realized with horror that he knew this time that *she* knew who he was.

She was too terrified to scream as she watched him switch off the tri-light lamp. His gloved hands circled her neck and he pressed her down on the sofa.

"Wanna make it, baby?" he asked her in his scared trembling voice.